SYNDICATE WOMAN

by

CHARLES NUETZEL

WRITING AS "JOHN DAVIDSON"

The Borgo Press
An Imprint of Wildside Press

MMVII

CONTENTS

INTRODUCTION

There are many ways of getting ideas for a story. Some writers wait for inspiration. Others find ideas diving in at them from all directions, drowning their ability to pick one idea over another. Some wait very, very long periods of time for that momentary instant when the mental light bulb pops brightly in their creative well and inspires another masterpiece.

That latter choice is not used by a full-time free-lance writer. Well, seldom, anyway!

A very famous song writer stated that his answer concerning "where do you get your ideas" was when the phone rings. Meaning, simply: he didn't worry about such matters until somebody called to give him an assignment for a new song.

Well, the free-lance writer is in much the same position. When the phone rings it is best to be ready with a number of ideas. Or be able to invent one on the spot, based on the publisher's immediate needs.

I had a simple trick I used under almost all conditions when I sat down to write: find a destination, a concluding point, then make a list of characters, and then begin writing the opening scene. I would start with a couple of people who in their conversation and action reveal to the reader the basic plot issues that will drive these people down a road that won't end until the last period of the story. I started by writing a neat, well-rounded narrative hook, a paragraph or so that would catch the reader's attention and hook them with a cute little snapper.

In this case I had an opening that set things up, and I knew exactly, generally speaking, where I'd be heading; and then I let my characters be presented on the set—paper—and let them do their thing.

A woman had been murdered in her bedroom. And Robert Bradley was determined to find those responsible! He came to Hollywood to learn the truth.

To his shock he learned that the dead woman had said:

> *"Hollywood is a horrible snare for young women like us. If you get in the right crowd you sleep your way up to fame. If you get in the wrong crowd, you sleep your way down into the gutter. If you're lucky you get some permanent relationship like mine. And what happens? It's a trap, too. The worst kind of trap. Because you can't get out; you can't get what you came to Hollywood for in the first place. So I'm a high class little prostitute. That's what all of us are!"*

Into this world Robert Bradley probed until he became a danger to powerful men. If he got too close they would kill him, too.

Murder, revenge, and passion mix to expose the

call-girl racket and strip it down to its raw bones—a nasty look at the beautiful, expensive young women and the price they pay as high class prostitutes that only rich men can afford.

—CHARLES NUETZEL
Thousand Oaks, California
August 2006

CHAPTER ONE

Robert Bradley looked down at the nude form of his wife lying on the bed next to him. *She is a hell of a beautiful woman*, he thought.

Her breasts were large and full, pick tipped and rigid, even though she was on her back. Her eyes were half closed, but even then they seemed large and innocent. She had the most beautiful figure he had ever seen on a woman.

It didn't seem possible that they were finally married. Regardless of the fact that they'd known each other for years—most of their lives. She was the first woman he'd ever had. They'd always planned to get married, but then....

When Carol had turned seventeen, the urge to become a movie star with her name in Big Lights had been too strong for her. The high school Talent Show and Drama class play had proven to her beyond any doubt that she had great talent and would take the film world by storm.

First it had been just wishing; dreaming to see *the big city of the stars*. Then when she had turned eighteen the desire became overwhelming. After graduating from high school she'd gone off to Hollywood. That was ages ago.

It amazed Robert to realize how long it *had*

9

been. Almost ten years. Ten long years of waiting.

A lot of things had happened to them both during that time. For him there had been four years in the Air Force. Traveling all over the world. That had been *his* means of escaping all the things that reminded him of Carol in the town where they had grown up. His was of getting a real thick slice of life.

Then coming back to Boise, he had gone into partnership with a friend running a small air field just outside of town. A lot had happened. He felt a pang of pity for another person—a woman, their secretary. The woman he was dating before Carol returned to live with her parents.

But that was life. He'd known Carol for years, and Norma for only a few months. Actually nothing more than one of many such affairs he'd enjoyed over the years.

"What are you thinking?" Carol asked in a low, almost child-like voice.

He looked down at her, gazing into her wide, innocent eyes. Reaching out a hand, he tenderly caressed her forehead, letting his fingers run into the light blonde locks of hair.

"Thinking about us. All the things that have happened." He paused and then continued: "I was thinking about what I had done after you left...but you never say anything about *your* life in Hollywood. Ten years, almost. Ten years that you won't share!"

"They weren't mine to share with you!" she said, half bitterly. Her eyes silently pleaded for him to change the subject, then looked away, avoiding him.

10

"What in the world does that mean?"

"Nothing. Oh, nothing. Let's not talk about *that!*" she stated almost sharply. Like she always did when he brought up the subject. Her past was a dark secret that she kept locked up inside, refusing to offer more than a glimmer. A vague comment about Hollywood being a tough game. Maybe someday she'd open up.

He didn't say anything for a moment. He had the feeling that Carol was ashamed of what had taken place in Hollywood. She always avoided comment concerning those years. But she had been changed by her experiences—that much he knew. More bitter; more hardened. But then, he wasn't a kid, either. He'd seen the whole world. The suffering. They both had changed a lot; and maybe that was good, because if one of them hadn't matured then they might not have been able to fall in love with each other again. And that had happened so very fast. One day she had called him. It was an openly "aggressive move" as she said it over the phone.

"I was hoping you weren't married," she announced the moment he recognized her voice.

A choke had lumped in his throat and it was difficult to get rid of it.

"I thought," she continued, quite bright and confident, "we might get together for dinner or something. Talk over old times. I've been in town for a couple of weeks. I checked with a few friends. Horrid of me, wasn't it? A terribly aggressive move, me calling you like this. But I simply had to look you up. Could we?"

That's when his voice returned. "Carol. My

God. I can't believe it."

"What's there to believe?"

"You visiting the old home town. That sophisti-
cated Hollywood lady..."

"Oh, poo, forget all that. I'm here to stay. Well,
at least, if it is possible to pick up my life."

"What happened?" he inquired, "didn't it work
out?"

"Nothing works out like we dream when we're
kids."

"What happened?" He wanted to know everything. All at once.

"Oh, nothing of interest. Really. I don't want to
talk about it, to be truthful."

"Married?"

"No. Never went there."

"Oh."

"I heard you almost got married a couple of
times."

"No, not really. Just dated. I guess you'd call
them affairs. Nothing lasting or totally serious."

"That's not what I've heard."

"Well, you simply heard rumors and junk like
that. Isn't what happened."

"People talk, but what do they know?" he offered. He didn't dare say what he was feeling at that
moment. He had never fallen out of love with Carol.
Through he hardly expected things to return to
where they were so many years ago. Teenage
crushes and love affairs were one thing, adult rela-
tionships another. They certainly were strangers,
now. Even though it didn't seem like that. "When
can we get together?"

"Is tonight too soon?" she asked. "I really think

it would be wonderful meeting you again. Maybe...wonder if we've changed too much."

Too much for what? He didn't even dare let himself consider that. Yet the question nagged his brain like a spear rammed into place, or a brand burned into his brain: *was there a chance they could pick up from where they had left off?*

He was surprised by that. The implications were obvious. He never had a chance to think much about them—for from that moment on he was on a roller coaster ride that kept on going for weeks. That very first night they'd gone out for dinner and then ended up having breakfast in bed in his house. The very bed they were now in. The instant they had seen one another it was obvious what would happen. And that very next morning in bed he knew that they would be together from then on. A few weeks later they'd gotten married. It was all a whirl wind, without stop, thought or consideration of anything other than the thrilling reality that nothing basically had changed, other than a resounding return to the feelings they'd shared years before for one another—plus her interest in an acting career totally gone. All she wanted to do was settle down and raise a family with him. Nothing else seemed to matter.

And that's all he had ever thought he wanted.

He refocused his gaze on Carol. She was smiling up at him, her eyes sparkling.

"You know..." she started to say, "I...I have a...surprise for you."

"What?" He jerked up in bed. It was past midnight.

She looked down, shyly. "I...I just wanted to wait for the right time to tell you. I wanted to drop it into the conversation so that you'd *really* be surprised."

"What are you talking about?" he asked.

She struggled with the words. "What I'm trying to say is that if I suddenly want...want pickles and ice cream or something like that—in the middle of the night..."

Robert suddenly jumped up in bed. His face lit up. "You're kidding!"

She nodded her head up and down, excitedly. "The doctor said in around eight months, from what he could tell!"

"A boy!" Robert said, excitedly.

"How do you know?"

"It better be!"

"But I want a girl!" she teased.

He looked slightly disappointed. "Okay, then— it can be a girl! But she better look like her mother!"

They laughed and she pulled him down toward the cushions of her full breasts. Then after a while they weren't thinking of babies!

The flood of desire; the heat of ecstatic excitement; the lava flow of burning sensual union. All moved through them, churning their forms. Thrashing them to a peak and then blowing them over the mountain cliff and down into the valley of peaceful rest below!

* * * * * * *

Robert didn't know how long he had slept before Carol woke him.

"What's wrong. dear?" he asked.

"I thought I heard a sound outside."

14

"I'll go check," he said, slipping out of bed. Reaching for his bathrobe he put it on and then moved from the room, without looking back at Carol.

He'd just gotten to the front door when he heard the sound of glass breaking. At first he couldn't make out in what direction it had come.

Then he heard a scream.

Carol's voice!

"Bob!" It was filled with terror and hopelessness, as if for some reason she were shouting his name for the last time!

Then there was the sound of gunfire.

Not one bullet. Not five, but a splattering sound of a sub-machine gun!

Robert was already rushing forward; and even when he heard the gun fire he didn't stop.

He ran into the bedroom, then came to a frozen halt.

Carol was lying outstretched on the bed. Her form twisted; her face distorted in the agony of death. Bloody holes were splattered all over her body. The bed was slowly turning crimson.

There was the sound of a car pulling away from the curb, but Robert didn't really hear it. He wasn't hearing anything at that moment. He was only conscious of one thing.

Carol was lying on the bed in a pool of her own blood—dead!

Then something snapped in his brain. All awareness slipped away. He moved without knowing what he was doing. He cried like a baby, without knowing he was doing it.

The police found him on the bed, the bloody,

twisted form of his wife clutched tightly against him. He was saying over and over again, "I love you. I won't let you die. I love you. I won't let you die. I love you. I won't let you die!

CHAPTER TWO

Robert Bradley wasn't conscious of having the doctor put the needle in his arm. He wasn't aware of slowly falling to sleep. The next thing that he knew was awakening in bed.

Awareness came slowly. First he turned, and gently moved his arm out to caress Carol. When he didn't feel her in bed next to him, his first thought was that she had gotten up already.

Then some inner consciousness started to move up his mind. He repelled it at first, refusing to admit the truth. *Something was wrong!* But he didn't want think about it. He refused to.

Carol! Carol, where are you! a frantic thought rushed through him.

He sat bolt upright in bed. His eyes wide open. His body was shaking.

Where was he?

"Where the hell...?" he cried out loud, looking at his surroundings.

He was in a strange room. A clean white room. It had the look of a hospital about it. Cold and hard.

He turned around and examined the bed. There was a buzzer attached to the bed-post. His hand moved toward it. Then he froze.

Don't push it! His emotions cried in terror.

17

What was wrong with him? Where was he? Where was Carol?

Carol! Carol had left him!

Carol was dead!

His mind revolted from that thought. His eyes closed tight to blot it out. But the thought remained.

Carol is dead.

Don't think that! I won't let her die!

But she is dead.

Suddenly he heard a screaming voice. It was high pitched. It came from nowhere. He couldn't make out from where it had come.

The scream sounded again.

"Carol! Carol! Don't die!" it said Then he realized that it was his own voice. It was a sobbing choking thing that racked through his whole body

Suddenly his hands were clamped against his face. His body was shaking

"No! Oh God no!" he choked out between trembling lips.

No! he screamed Abruptly he felt strong hands grip him. Then he felt a pain shoot through his arm.

Awareness slipped away.

Blackness clouded around him. It was a dark sea of endless peace. But there was an evilness about it. Something that his mind wouldn't think about. Something important that he knew he *had* to remember. But he couldn't.

* * * * * * *

The blackness cleared and then sharp light blinded his eyes.

He was sitting up in bed. Looking across the far

18

wall.

His body seemed to be numb. There wasn't any feeling at first. Then slowly it ebbed back. And with feeling came the awareness.

Carol is dead. She was shot to death with a submachine gun.

No!

I won't let her die!

Carol is dead!

That realization came with no emotion. It was simply a statement of fact. But the reaction he felt, because of that statement, was completely emotional.

He fought back the emotion. He fought back the rejection of what he now was forced to face as *truth.*

Carol is dead!

For a long time he sat there, not moving. His face white and drawn. No expression showed on it. It didn't indicate the inner torment going on inside his mind.

"Get hold of yourself, Bob!" he said. *Carol is dead. Nothing you can do will change that!*

He tried to force himself to accept that. But the more he fought the greater the emotional feeling welled inside him. It flooded over all sanity. It overwhelmed him. And abruptly he was aware of the screaming voice. That high pitched insane screaming he knew was coming from his own lungs.

Hands took hold of him. Slapped his face. The screaming changed to sobbing. Overwhelming sobbing.

He felt the needle in his arm.

Suddenly the world spun. There was silence for a long time and then abruptly the mist cleared and

19

he was lying on a bed and Carol was across the room, nude, looking at herself in the mirror.

She turned and looked at him, "Do you think that I'm beautiful, Robert?"

"Yes, God, how beautiful you are! As beautiful as a goddess!"

She smiled and turned toward him so that he could see her body. The rounded hips that curved smoothly down to long full thighs. Her breasts, rosy centered and full and erect. Her smile became all the sexual and passionate desire that he had always known when she was making love to him.

"You want me?" she asked, starting to move in his direction. Each step swung her hips delightfully. Each step jogged the points of her breasts.

"Oh, how I want you! Where have you been? Why have you gone away?" he cried in a choking voice.

"But I haven't been away. You've been in my thoughts all along. I've been in your thoughts. And as long as you think about me, I'll always be with you!"

She slid down next to him, reaching for his hands and moving them up to her breasts. Her lips parted and a sigh of delighted pleasure floated from her throat.

"Oh, take me, dearest! Take me!" she cried, clawing at him.

Then they embraced. He felt her body against his.

"Oh, Robert, I love you so much! So very, very much! So very, very much!"

A convulsive shudder rushed through her as he pushed against her. He felt her stomach muscles re-

20

spond to his nearness. Her hands clawed at his back. Her teeth bit into his shoulder as she moved in ecstatic pleasure

Finally it was over and they were lying on a beach, looking up at the sun.

"Where have you been?" he asked.

"Don't you know?"

"No!" he said softly.

"Well, I won't tell you. It will make you unhappy and I want to feel you in my arms again!"

She moved to him, her body pressing tightly. Her lips kissed his cheek and his neck and then moved to his mouth. He felt her hands slide around his neck and the gentle pressure of them caressing tenderly.

Then abruptly she broke away and a sad expression clouded her features.

"What's wrong?" he cried.

"I have to go," she said, tears coming into her eyes

Where? Where?

"Back."

"Where? Why? Don't leave me!"

"I don't want to leave you!"

"Where are you going?" he demanded angrily, pulling her against him

"Back to death!" she whispered in his ear

Then suddenly he heard the sound of a submachine gun. A stickiness seemed to well between them. He stepped back and saw bloody holes searing Carol's beautiful naked body.

She smiled at him. "You know that I was killed. Just kiss me before I leave. Just kiss me again, please!"

21

He cried out in horror, stepping back.

Carol's arms reached out for him, but he turned and ran. Ran through the gathering mists. Through the ugly fog that was rushing in around him. He screamed and screamed, then sudden blackness clouded around his awareness.

And he awoke.

He knew that Carol was dead. His eyes opened.

He felt nothing at first. Only the emptiness a person knows when everything has been pulled out from under him.

There was no reason to live. No feeling. There was nothing.

He sat there, trying to *feel*. Trying to *react*. Wanting to cry. Wanting to scream. Wanting to...

But nothing.

A hard shell had settled over him.

He turned and reached for the buzzer and rang it. A few moments later a nurse walked in. She looked at him with a serious expression on her face for a moment, then she smiled.

"Well, how are we feeling?" she asked, stepping to the side of the bed taking his wrist.

He just nodded. He didn't say anything for a while; he couldn't think of anything to say. Then finally when she had finished he asked, "When can I get out of here?"

She looked at him, a strange expression on her face. "That depends on the doctor—and you."

"I want out!" he said in an even, emotionless voice.

"We'll see."

"Get the doctor!"

"He'll be around in an hour or so!"

For a moment a slight emotion welled in him, but he fought it back, knowing what it would bring; knowing all the grief and hurt and sorrow...

Forcing himself to relax, he lay back in bed and said: "Okay, when he gets here. Just tell him I want out of this place!"

He lay there for a long time without thinking. He didn't dare think. Thinking would be dangerous. He knew that much. So he lay there thinking about *not* thinking.

Suddenly the doctor was standing over him. "How are you feeling today?"

He opened his eyes. The man standing there was tall and elderly. His face was kind.

"I want out!"

The doctor smiled and nodded. "I see that you're feeling better."

"I want out!" he said evenly.

"We'll see. We'll see!"

"I want out, *today!*" he told the doctor.

The man looked at the nurse, nodded and then walked out. The nurse followed him, returning a little later with a couple of pills and a small cup of water.

"Take these," she said.

He didn't resist. He didn't *care* about anything except getting out as soon as possible. There was something that he had to do. What it was he didn't know. There was just an inner awareness that there was something very important to do; and that he couldn't do it in the hospital.

He lay there trying to think about it. But his mind wouldn't bring it to the surface of his thoughts; as if it were afraid of letting him know about its secret.

When the time comes, he thought, *I'll know. But don't think about it right now.*

*Don't think...*he was getting sleepy. The thoughts came slowly, mixed, and without any order or logic. Then finally they stopped completely.

He didn't dream. He just woke up in the middle of the night. All was blackness around him. All was quiet.

He felt emotionally numb, in a kind of lovely daze that made it possible to think logically, coolly, without being drained in any way. It was like looking through a clear glass, but the window was there between him and the hurt. It was possible to be rational and to act.

He suddenly knew what it was he had to do; why he had to get out of the hospital!

Why had Carol been killed? What had caused it! Who was responsible?

Slowly he got out of bed. There was a window off to one side of the room. He crept quietly over to it. Then he reached out and pulled it open.

He threw one leg over the sill. Then the other leg. He climbed slowly and quietly out. He looked down at the ground a few feet below; and jumped.

He had to find the people responsible for his wife's death, He had to find them and kill them...

The people, he felt sure, lay in her past; the past ten years in Hollywood.

That was where he would find out the answers.

He walked off slowly into the night, keeping in the shadows; heading in the direction of his home. There was where he would start. That's where the trail would begin.

24

* * * * * * *

He'd been in his house for half an hour, looking and searching through his wife's papers. Looking for a clue; some hint of where to start in Hollywood.

Anything. An address. A letter. Something that might give him a lead. He needed a starting point, and from there he knew it wouldn't be long before he was heading toward his wife's murderer.

There weren't many things to look through. His wife hadn't brought much. No letters that gave any hint of her past life. No real communications.

Then finally he found one simple clue. The name of a woman. It was written on the back of a napkin. *Ruth Kirby.* That was all; but it might be a beginning. There was one other thing. A match box. From a nightclub or restaurant called *Tropical City.* That might be another lead.

It would be a beginning, that much he knew.

He walked from the room and then into the kitchen. Going to the cupboard he pulled down a bottle of whiskey and poured himself a strong shot.

He gulped half of it and then went into the bathroom. He got out of the hospital pajamas and into the shower. Fifteen minutes later he was stepping from the bathroom. It only took a few minutes to dress. Then he downed the rest of the whiskey, and after checking his wallet to make sure he had enough money, he walked outside.

For a moment he stood looking at the place where he and Carol had spent a little over one short month of happiness together. Then he walked to the garage and got into his car. It would be a long drive to Hollywood; a long drive that would give him plenty of time to think things out; to make plans.

* * * * * * *

It took him three days to get to Hollywood. And every day was driven through in a terrible daze. It all seemed like a nightmare from which he couldn't escape. All that kept him going was the determination to discover who had been responsible for his wife's brutal murder. What would happen then, he didn't even try to plan out. Revenge was prime—but how to get it was another manner. He knew too damned little. And the more he thought about it the more difficult it was to keep from feeling this was a terrible dream that would never end.

The desert trip was long and tiring, hot and only relieved when he came through Los Angeles proper—a huge sprawling landscape. Hollywood was just a little further, within the county.

It was a strange city to him; an alien city that could only mean one thing: revenge for his wife's death.

Checking into a hotel he ordered a drink brought to his room and then looked up the address of Ruth Kirby, the only possible link between himself and the killers.

He had just found the phone number when the drink was brought. He tipped the bell-boy, downed part of the liquor. Then he picked up the receiver and dialed Ruth Kirby's number.

The line was busy.

He dialed the number once more. Still busy. Lying back, he finished the drink and then closed his eyes. *There is plenty of time,* he thought sleepily. *After all, he had waited this long. Maybe he could use a little sleep. No! Try the phone one more time!*

He sat up and dialed. The busy signal greeted him again.

The world clouded around him before he was aware of it. The blackness. And then an inner awareness that Carol was near him. That she was very close. He could smell the perfume. The delightful scent of her body as it smelled while lying close to him in bed.

He turned and saw her lying there, next to him.

"Carol, you've returned!" he cried, pulling closer to her and reaching out a hand to caress her naked breasts. A sigh uttered past her lips. Her arms reached out and circled his neck, her delicate fingers caressing, urging him to continue, to make tender love to her.

"Oh, you're so good," she sighed in his ear as his hands slid around her back. She trembled in his arms, sobbing.

Carol's face started wrinkling before his eyes. The skin started to shrivel against the skull, it stretched away from the bone, breaking and tearing, exposing the whiteness underneath. Moments later he was looking into the face of a grinning skull!

"You see, I'm dead," it said, hollowly. "I'm dead and in the ground and you can't have me any more. *You can never have me anymore...*"

CHAPTER THREE

It was one of those typical parties she had to attend from time to time. The kind she hated, and the kind that also built the business. The room was getting crowded with desperately anxious men, some young enough, most rather middle-aged, thick around the middle and a few with balding head and graying hair. The typical business mix of eager young execs. It didn't matter what kind of business; all were much the same. Conventions or business meetings. Or simply the loving Hollywood set who couldn't get their eyes, nor hands, off the lovely young ladies who desperately sought careers in films.

It didn't matter. All were the same to her.

Ruth Kirby looked with mixed emotions at the man who was coming toward her. Jake Turner. She hated him; and yet found herself attracted to the animal side of this brute. Not that he was good looking, but he knew how to make love to a woman! He knew which buttons to push!

And one thing Ruth could say about herself was that she could easily be sent into fits of desire. All that any man had to do was push the right buttons. If they didn't it was fake-city for her. But Jake knew how to do it better than most!

"What are you doing, Ruthie?" Jake asked as he stepped up to her.

She automatically smiled at him. He merely grinned.

He was as obvious as a baboon in a monkey house full of crazed, passionate female monks. She thought of Jake as a savage homo sap! A stupid, brutal ape.

"It's been a long time," he commented, looking down at the large dip between her breasts.

She could finish that line for him: *Since we've been in bed together!* And it excited her. That was the most annoying part about this man. She found him erotically thrilling.

"It's been a long time, Jake. Too long. What's new?"

He raised his hands helplessly. "The same old thing. You know how it is. Gotta keep busy."

*Busy watching out for the call-girl rackets and the racing and numbers rackets and the...*She let the thought trail off.

"Have somebody I want you to meet, Ruthie!" he said, taking hold of her arm and pulling her forward. "A girl that I want you to take in as a roommate."

She felt herself tense.

Another one of those, she thought bitterly. Another young girl wanting to get into show business; some young thing who came from the sticks with stars in her eyes. The bright stars would be changed to dull hard ice in a few months! A few months of men pawing her and taking her to bed and using her body! All in the name of survival and in the illusion it would get her somewhere in the Industry. Some crap that was!

"What this time?" she asked, letting Jake lead her through the crowd.

"Same as before. Just play her around. You know...see that she gets the right *outlook* on things. Then you can turn her over to the 'boys' and they'll do the rest."

That meant to convince the poor girl that you couldn't get anywhere in Hollywood unless you were willing to "play ball" with the right men. Then she would be loaned out to the little "inner circle." After they had gotten through stringing her along she would be turned over to the *real* market-boys and from then on she'd be just another "starlet"; except with a special title: *"Call Girl!"*

It could be a dirty racket. But on the other hand, if it worked out right, a girl could make a lot of money, and some actually retired rich. Those were the lucky ones. Still, a better alternative to being nothing but a casting couch toy, tossed from couch to couch, with the only payoff being lousy lies, empty promises that ended most of the young girls as street whores, desperately attempting to survive in a city that simply didn't give a damn.

At least the call-girl racket could be a better way for many of the starry eyed, silly little lovely girls who sought fame and fortune in show business. The competition in the film industry, the acting profession, was harsh and demanding and haunted by selfishly obsessed actors. And too many wannabees. The successful ones usually ended up stomping on anything that got in their way. A dirty business. Not much cleaner than the one she was now in.

Finally Jake Turner came to a stop before a

beautiful young redhead.

"Ruth, this is June Edmondson."

The redhead nodded, smiling.

"Glad to know you," she said, extending her hand.

"I want you two girls to get to know each other real well. You're to stay with Ruth, June. She'll be able to tell you a lot of things...tips on how to get along—and *ahead*." Before either woman could say anything, Jake quickly added. "Give her your address, Ruth, and phone number. She'll be able to get in touch with you later in the week."

Ruth did as she was told, quickly and without comment. Then Jake took a strong grip on her arm and said: "Now, come along with me. It's been a long time since we've had a chance to *visit*. I have a few things to talk to you about."

They moved across the room, away from June, and then into a small study. There were a few people standing around, talking. A small bar-cabinet was in the corner. Jake moved her in that direction.

"I think you need another drink, dearie," he announced.

She needed a drink like a hole in the head; but she was being told—not asked.

His hands moved with expert care, as his lips repeated the story that he always told while mixing drinks: "You know, the secret of a good drink is to make it taste good, and at the same time very effective. Now you take a shot of gin, a shot of vodka and a dash of lime juice—then a little liqueur. Pour it over the ice and stir it around a little...and you have a cocktail!" He handed her a glass filled full with reddish liquid. "To you, my dear!" he announced, tapping her glass with his. Then he took several strong sips of his drink.

She just touched her lips to the cocktail.

"Okay, Jake. What's the bit?" she asked softly.

He looked sharply at her for a moment. "You know, Ruth, you are quite a woman!"

He stared at her for a long time. Then, tapping her shoulder, he nodded in the direction of an inner office.

"In there." His voice was suddenly very serious.

She followed him, without saying anything.

He closed the door behind them, and then moved to a small desk that was centered on the far wall. Stepping around it he motioned her into a chair opposite his. For a moment he didn't say anything, just looked carefully at her.

She fingered the glass nervously and looked down at it; then looked up again, as he started speaking.

"Ruthie, you've been around this town for quite a spell. You know the score. You're not a fool. You've had a lot of hard knocks. And most of all: you know damned well who to play ball with—*and how to do it!*"

He paused and she silently nodded.

"I was in New York for a purpose. I stayed there for several months for a purpose. A good one. There are big things about to happen. Very big." He stopped again, staring carefully at her. "You understand what I'm leading up to?"

She shook her head. "Not exactly. But I'm listening."

He took a swallow of his drink and then said: "We screen people carefully. We make sure that we know what kind of a person they are."

"What are you trying to say, Jake?"

"Simply that there's a big change about to take place. And if you're interested..."

He let it lay there. His hands spread.

She thought that over for a moment. It wasn't any patty-cake party that he was talking about. She'd been working for him for some time, now, but only as a member of the outer circle. Not the inner core. Now he was asking her if she was interested in getting in deep. And getting in deep meant two things: one, there would be big money involved; two, the element of danger was bigger, not only from the law, but from the Syndicate.

"I'm listening," she commented dryly, taking a strong sip of her drink.

"I was talking with the Syndicate boys. The big ones. There was a lot of talk. And a lot of plans made. And now those plans are going into operation." He stopped and looked sharply at her, his eyes narrowing, his lips tightening. "If you step across this line—you don't back out. *Ever!*"

She became the cold business woman. "How much money in it?"

"Who talks about money at times like this?" He smiled; it was a silky, oily smile that had all the danger of a snake. And the brute force of a gorilla in heat.

"I do!"

"Okay, then. I can give you...just an idea." He thought for a moment. "One: this is a multi-million dollar deal that we're entering into. It will take something like six or seven months before it will be ready for you to do anything. But it should bring

you into the six figure bracket per year; top numbers, too. At least. And that could be after expenses.
All tax free. More if things go well."

The mask of her face showed no emotion.
"What do I have to do to make that kind of money?'

"The same thing you've been doing. But on a
much larger scale."

She sighed, rather seriously. "You mean the
whoring racket, prostitution..."

"The Call Girl racket! Come on, you know better than that!" he announced in a grand manner.

"Some times, Jake, I just feel the need to call it
as it is!"

"Call girl, escort service, running a house, pimp-
ing, madam, hell, Ruth, why quibble?"

"The only difference between all that is degree.
We're pimps, grand and wonderful and all that, big
dealers and all that, but not any better—other than
the money—than those who run the street whores.
And you know it, Jake!" she announced rather
coldly.

"You always have been a hard one!" he managed to smile that off. "But we're talking big, big
bucks, and you know it."

"I understand. And didn't say I wasn't interested." She hated it all, but was realistic enough to
understand the realities of life. "So...what's the
deal?"

"To put it simply: you'll be in charge of han-
dling *personnel*. But on a grand scale compared to
what you've been involved with up until now. "

"Why me?"

"Because you have shown great ability in turning so-called nice young girls into the type of

women that we like. Cooperative ladies willing to flop for quick big bucks. You have a way about you. You're intelligent. A good business woman. You've played ball with us...the way we like it." He stopped, taking a deep breath. "That's all I can tell you right now. Until you decide to commit. No answers right now. Think it over."

She knew what it meant. The Syndicate was organizing a nation-wide deal. A *new* deal. A more organized deal. Something vaster than it already had. What, she couldn't really guess. Only that it was big, and she was being offered a thin slice of it!

"I know the answer now," she said carefully.

"Think about it!" he told her, standing.

"Okay, I'll think. But I'll be saying, *yes!*"

He nodded knowingly. "Think about it, anyway. There's no hurry to have the answer—yet. Right now we're feeling a few people out. A few *key* people like yourself."

Then after a short silence he smiled at her. "It's sure been a long time..." He let his voice drift off, and his eyes lowered in the direction of her neckline.

"You know, Jake, how I feel about you," she said in a husky voice. "Why play around? We know what you want."

"Just me? What about you and that lush, wanton body?"

"Okay, what *we* want!" she offered, with a smile, knowing that's what he needed to hear.

He walked around the desk. "Yes, I've always said that you were quite a girl!"

His hand reached around her waist and pulled her tightly to him.

35

"Let's go up to my room," he said.

She smiled and looked toward the sofa. "Why? You have everything a girl would need right here."

A low chuckle sounded from his barrel chest and then he moved across the room. "I'll go get some drinks, and you can get...you know what!"

Even though her body was suddenly burning to be taken by Jake, there was the inner disgust that she felt for herself. This was cheap, and she knew it. But she really couldn't care; she was a slave to her desires and there wasn't anything she could do about it! She was a woman who would take any-thing offered to her, any time and any place! Right now the place was Jake's private office.

What the hell difference did it really make? she thought bitterly, starting to remove her dress.

As she was sitting on the sofa, with only her bra and panties on, Jake stepped into the room, a bottle of whiskey in his hand. He closed and locked the door, then settled down next to her, handing her a drink.

"Bottoms up!" he laughed, patting her thigh.

Ruth felt a stab of excitement at the contact of his hand on her naked flesh. She wanted to hungrily claw him to her, but she knew that there was such a thing as the right time. First the drinks, then the sex. That's how it always was.

It took only a few minutes to gulp down the drinks, and all the time Jake was caressing her thigh with his fingers, while his eyes were undressing her. But finally the torture was over and he reached roughly for her, crushing her to him.

His lips ground onto hers, as his hands reached around and started working on the clasp of her bra.

36

It came deftly loose in his expert fingers. Then all at once he was fondling and caressing her until she thought that she'd go mad with desire.

"Oh, *God!*" she moaned between clenched teeth, clawing at his back. Her lips sought his and she felt the probing moistness of his tongue as it touched her, rhythmically. She hated it; and loved it.

They held each other a long time, then his lips started circling around toward her throat, and she felt the dig of his teeth as he nibbled on the lobe of her ear; then he began to circle his lips downwards. Finally they were caressing her shoulder. She felt the moistness of his tongue working between his teeth; then they slid down and along the upper swell of her breast. After that she wasn't conscious of anything except the rapidly building swell of pleasure that whipped her body from side to side, until she couldn't stand it! Until she screamed in savage pain-filled ecstasy!

How long she lay, relaxed and satisfied, before she became aware of things around her, she didn't know. But when she opened her eyes she saw Jake standing over her, completely dressed, looking at the curving design of her body.

"You're good. Real good. And you sure liked it, didn't you?" he observed in a voice that exposed the pride he was feeling. It was a silly ego-game he always played. He wanted the woman to praise his wonderful bedroom style. Gorilla-style.

"Of course," she said, slightly irritated by his attitude. Slowly she stood and started getting dressed. When she was finished she fixed herself a drink and after downing it quickly she turned to Jake. "Yes, you were very good. That much I have to give you!"

He laughed and then said: "Well, the party is over—in here, for the night. There are a few things I have to take care of...I really shouldn't even have taken the time.... But *you* know how that is, baby! My heart throbs for you!"

That's not the only thing that throbs, she thought with bitter amusement.

She nodded and turned to leave.

"I'll see you tomorrow night," he said, as she moved to the door.

"Why not?" she said over her shoulder, closing the door behind her. She couldn't help feeling a sense of personal defeat. She had gone to his arms like a helpless child; yet there was nothing she could do about it—now or ever! She was gorilla meat to his demands. It was both business and personal, even if she disliked the man.

Ten years ago she'd come to Hollywood to get into the movies. It was the world-wide old story: a young girl finding out that life wasn't as simple as it appeared on the surface. She'd never made a picture—but there'd been a lot of men. One hell of a lot of men! And now she was in with the inner circle that ran a nice little ring of ladies as escorts for business men and for so-called Hollywood big wigs. In actual fact it was a call-girl racket that some of the young women actually believed to be a stepping stone to a career in acting. They learned, soon enough, the trap they'd fallen into. But once in, there was hardly any easy way out. Everybody made good money, even the girls. As for herself, she had a cover business, which was an office to go to, where she made sure everything was run smoothly. Jake was her boss, even if he kept out of the office. She appeared, for all practical purposes, to be self-employed.

She looked around the room, scanning the people with her eyes. Then she spotted the woman called June Edmondson. Her *new* room-mate. The girl was talking to a man Ruth didn't recognize but there was a look on the young woman's face that showed a desperate boredom.

Ruth felt sorry for her. A young starlet. A young woman about to be changed into a call girl. The innocence, the dreamer, would be shattered, crushed, molded into something more flexible and realistic. Some of it would be new lies to feed her childishly young mind. But it all was just a matter of changing one lie for different one, something that would, in the long run, bring more money.

She walked over.

"Excuse me," she said, "But could I talk to you?"

She directed the question to June.

The woman looked relieved. She smiled frozenly at the man and said. "I'm sorry...."

Then she walked across the room with Ruth.

"I was wondering," Ruth said, "If maybe you might like to move into my place, tonight?"

She paused in order to examine the reaction on the other's face.

"I *am* rather...bored."

Ruth laughed: "These parties are really dull!" Then she became serious. "Look, why don't you come over to my place and give it a look-see. Then you can stay there this evening. Tomorrow we can arrange to have your things moved over."

Jane's eyes brightened. "That might be nice!"

"Then it's settled!" Ruth announced, heading toward the bedroom where all the coats were hung. "Let's get out of here!"

CHAPTER FOUR

Robert Bradley woke suddenly. He jerked up in bed, the dream still painful in his mind. That horrible dream that had ended so terribly.

Why had he dreamed twice about his dead wife? He reached for the phone and dialed. The phone rang.

Three. Four. Five. Six times.

He hung up. Reaching for a pack of cigarettes, he pulled one out and lighted it. Taking a deep drag he moved to the small bathroom and looked at himself in the mirror.

His face stared back, drawn and white. Tired.

Putting the cigarette down, he washed and then after taking a strong drag from the cigarette again, put it out. He really didn't like smoking. Just that right now he was so unhinged. He walked to the phone and dialed again. No answer.

Sighing, he moved across the room, opened the door and stepped into the hall.

A few minutes later he was in the small coffee shop eating breakfast.

Half an hour later he was back in his room once more, dialing Ruth Kirby's number.

This time there was an answer.

"Hello?" a bright, young sounding voice asked.

"This Mr. Bradley, Miss Kirby—you don't..."

"I'm not Miss Kirby."

"Oh?' He felt nervous.

"She's out right now. Can I tell her you called?"

He thought about that and then said: "When do you expect her?"

"In about half an hour to an hour."

"Okay. Thanks." He said good-bye and hung up.

There was only one way to get things moving fast. He'd look her name up again and then get the address. Go out to her place. On the phone she could make things difficult—if she wanted to. In person he would be able to get more information from her—if there was information to get.

He got her address from the telephone book, then walked from the room out to his car.

Half an hour later he was parking across the street from a large, modem white apartment house on Wilshire, in Westwood Village.

Then he was knocking on apartment number 17.

The door opened almost right away. A young red-head looked out. A surprised expression crossed her features.

"Oh, I thought that was Ruthie!" she sighed in a light voice.

He couldn't help noticing the beautiful full shape of her figure, the wide, innocent eyes. She looked like a kitten. Beautiful little kitten.

"I'm Mr. Bradley," he said. "Are you...?"

"June Edmondson. Come on in, Mr. Bradley, you can wait here for Ruth."

The apartment Robert stepped into was modern from the word go. It had low Chinese furniture, white and black. A large mirror on the far wall; a small bar in the corner. It looked expensive. The woman whom he had come to see seemed to have money, and plenty of it—or a man to keep her.

"Sit down, make yourself at home, Mr. Bradley."

He sat. His eyes accidentally made contact with the woman's figure. He didn't look on purpose; beautiful women were the last things he was interested in now. There was only one woman for him— and she lay dead!

He forced himself not to think about Carol. He didn't want to think about what he'd lost. His wife—and a coming baby!

The pain ebbed up like a volcanic wave, which he desperately fought back, putting a hard wall between his feelings that those attempting to erupt. First anger welled, then terrible anguish, then a hard edge of control set into place.

Bitterness showed on his face for a moment. Then he forced himself to focus on June Edmondson's figure.

Look at anything! Think about anything—except Carol!

This was a beautiful young woman. A body that was well formed and shapely. High pointing breasts looked firm and full. Hips were round and circling. And what he could see of her legs was intriguing!

She smiled slightly under his gaze. "Would you like a drink?"

He thought about that for a moment and then nodded. He suddenly felt a strong need for one.

June moved across the room toward the small bar. With each step her hips made a little swaying motion. It was quite natural; actually charming.

After a few moments she moved back and handed him a tall highball.

"I hope she doesn't mind," June said, smiling slightly over the rim of her glass.

"Who?"

"Ruth. I just moved in today. This morning. There wasn't much to move—really. But she said to make myself at home. Take anything I wanted. So..." She took a sip of her drink, her gaze keeping on him. There was interest showing in those blue eyes.

Robert forced himself to look away, taking a strong swallow of the high-ball. It was a powerful drink, he realized, taking another gulp. Exactly what he needed.

Just then there was the sound of a key sliding into the lock of the front door, which opened and a tall woman in her early thirties stepped in. At first she didn't notice Robert. When she did, she stopped short, surprise showing on her face. Then she gained control of her features and glided forward.

"I didn't know that you had connected with a man so soon, June," she said, surprise in her voice.

June looked bewildered, 'Oh, but he's not...he came to see *you.*"

"Oh?" Ruth turned toward Robert. There was a cold careful look about her stare. Then she became all business. "Who're you?"

June spoke first. "Mr. Bradley, I thought you knew him...I'm terribly sorry if—"

"Oh, be quiet!" Ruth snapped, angrily. Then she said: "What do you want?"

"I want to ask you a few questions."

"About what?"

"About Carol Benton. That was her name when she came to Hollywood about ten years ago. I saw your name in some of her papers."

No emotion showed on Ruth's face.

"You knew her?" asked Robert, his voice tense.

There was a little silence before she spoke. Then she sighed. "Yes, I knew her—a little."

"I have to find out the people she knew. The ones she ran around with."

"Why?"

"Because she's dead!"

There was a slight reaction on Ruth's face to that statement. Her eyes narrowed and then her lips pursed out for a second.

"She was killed!"

"Oh, *no!*" Ruth cried in a voice struck with emotion. "She was so—" Then she caught herself. "How'd it happen?"

"Somebody murdered her. I want to know who!" Bitterness was thickly in control of his voice.

There was a stunned silence. Ruth's mouth opened and then closed. Her eyes were wide with alarm. They were filled with concerned worry. And something else. Her mouth moved as if to speak, and then she closed it once more.

She stood there for a little longer and then slowly her body became rigid and the expression on her face tightened. It was as if she had suddenly put up a solid wall between herself and her emotional responses.

"I don't know...know why you think that I would know about it!" she snapped, a little angrily.

"Your name was in some of her papers," he said.

"Why that doesn't mean anything! A lot of women have my name." She paused for a moment and then continued. "After all, what do you expect me...I mean...how would I know anything about *that?*"

"I thought you might be able to tell me something about her other friends."

"I'm sorry. Really I am. I hardly knew her. Just once, a long time ago. She ran around with a man I knew...that's all"

"Who was it?"

"He's...he's...well, he's dead!"

Robert had the feeling that she was lying through her teeth. Her first reaction had been too intense, too strong, too overwhelming. Shock. Raw shock. There was something she wasn't telling. Something she was hiding. And there wasn't much that he could do about it. But he had to try. Something. Anything.

"You're lying!" he said evenly, without emotion.

Her reaction was startling. First surprise. Second fear. Third anger. "What right do you have to call me a liar! In *my* own apartment? What right! You get the hell out of here! And I mean it! Get the hell out! And don't ever come back. If you do, I'll have some of my friends make you wish that you had never...never...*just get out!* I can't help you. That's all there is to it! I'm sorry about your friend. But there's nothing that I can do to help you!"

Suddenly the anger became a little less sharp and there was a thin edge of concern half hidden under the emotion. "I'm really sorry...there's nothing that I can do to help you. Except to tell you—

46

just get out...forget about..." She stopped, abruptly seeming to realize what she *was* saying. Then anger returned. She didn't say anything. Just walked to the door and flung it open.

There wasn't anything he could do but walk out. Maybe later he would be able to see her. Maybe later she would be more willing to talk to him.

Maybe.

* * * * * * *

Fifteen minutes later he was driving along the Hollywood freeway, trying to decide what to do; where to turn next. There was the *Tropical City*. A restaurant. He could go there. But that was a very slim lead; possibly nothing. She might have gone there only once. She might never have been there. Some friend could have given her the matches. Yet that was the only thing that he had left to do. Except go back to Ruth Kirby's apartment and beat the holy hell out of her. And that was one thing he didn't like. He'd never struck a woman in his life before. But...

But he suddenly realized that he wouldn't stop short of *anything* to get at Carol's killers! Beating up a woman was nothing!

The thing he could always remember was: *there had been no reason for Carol to be killed—and whoever had done it hadn't been playing by the rule book! They'd played for keeps.*

Well, he was going to play for keeps too! Next stop:

Tropical City.

CHAPTER FIVE

The minute that Robert had stepped out of her apartment, Ruth went into her bedroom and closed the door. Then she stepped to the phone and dialed Jake Turner's number. There was a moment of silence and then the sound of ringing. After a few seconds someone picked up the receiver and said: "Hello."

"Can I speak to Mr. Turner?"

"Who is it?"

"Ruth Kirby."

There was a second of silence and then the voice said: "I'm sorry, Miss Kirby, but Mr. Turner is on the phone right now. Talking to New York. Can I have him call you?"

Ruth thought for a moment and then decided against the idea. "No...I'll get in touch with him...later."

Slowly she placed the receiver on the hook and sat numbly on the edge of the bed. An overture of thoughts was racing through her mind.

Carol dead. Carol dead. *Carol. Dead.*

Carol.

Dead.

She'd been so full of life.

Carol.

Dead!

Killed.

Murdered.

Fear moved through her. Fear caused by the thought that maybe *she* would end that way. The trouble with getting in with the big boys was that you *couldn't* get out. Carol had tried, but she'd ended up dead. *Murdered.*

Stop thinking! her mind cried in alarm. *Carol had known what she was getting into when she started*—or did she?

Ruth wondered if any of them ever really realized what they were doing. They got all wound up, twisted and trapped. It was a trap that slowly spun its spell; and before a girl knew what was happening she was caught and there wasn't any way out.

What was it that Carol had said once? Ruth tried to remember. It was something about...

"Hollywood is a horrible snare for young women like us. If you get in the right crowd you sleep your way up to fame. If you get in the wrong crowd, you sleep your way down into the gutter. If you're lucky you get some permanent relationship like mine. And what happens? It's a trap, too. The worst kind of trap. Because you can't get out; you can't get what you came to Hollywood for in the first place. So I'm a high class little prostitute. That's what all of us are!"

That had been one of her last swan songs. Carol had taken it as long as she could. A bitter defeat. The terrible knowledge that you're no good for anything but being some big shot's woman. No marriage. No chance to have a nice normal home with a nice normal husband.

49

Ruth had felt a terrible shock at seeing Robert Bradley in her apartment. She had recognized him right away. Carol had shown her his picture enough times. Robert Bradley, the man she had given up to become a Hollywood star. Only to become, instead, a Hollywood tramp—a Hollywood whore!

Ruth tried to force her mind away from those thoughts.

You're in too deep to do anything about it, now, she thought, bitterly.

Suddenly self-hate moved through her.

It had been a good thing that Jake Turner hadn't been able to answer the phone. She had been about to spring a dirty trap on Robert Bradley. And that wasn't right. He looked like a nice guy. He looked like a good man. There wasn't any reason for him to be killed.

He *would be*—that much she did know. He'd be killed, unless he got the hell out of Hollywood before he nosed around too much. The "boys" would see to it that he got stopped; and fast!

Slowly she stood. The best thing she could do— for the memory of Carol, at least—was to remain silent about what had happened in her apartment. If Robert Bradley wanted to get himself killed, that would be his own affair; but she wouldn't have anything to do with it!

Sighing, she walked into the front room. She would have to begin the slow training of June Edmondson. June Edmondson, young, small-town girl wanting to become a famous star. Getting her name in lights.

The only light that June would see would be the light of new understanding about the ways of the world! The light of bitterness; defeat; self-hate and disgust. The only fame she'd get was the amount she deserved for her ability to satisfy men in bed! The only kind of acting that she would do, would be to fool men into thinking that she liked their coarse caresses, their hammering bodies and searching hands. Fake it. Just like all too many wives faked it for their dumb husbands. Only in this business it was a continual fake-job, time and again, with an endless list of so-called lovers. June would soon become a part of the fake-it-squad.

But first Ruth would need a drink. A lot of drinks. She walked to the bar and poured herself a straight shot of whiskey.

Let Bradley take care of himself! Let Ruth take care of herself! Let June Edmondson take care of her "great wonderful career" as a Hollywood Call-girl—with Ruth's supervision!

Bitterly, Ruth looked at the girl and then downed the drink in one swallow.

CHAPTER SIX

Tropical City was one of those places where a person goes to be picked up, or to pick up somebody. A dive, in other words. In the service Robert had seen a lot of such places. Women acted as if they wanted "supermen" and that anybody who tried to make a pass at them was something lower than a worm. They would give a guy a slow cold stare, and then say they weren't interested, while all the time their pants were burning for a man.

Well, that was the way it usually turned out for guys who didn't know the score. Others were able to play the game and score readily.

He settled himself on a bar stool and motioned to the barman. "Give me a whiskey on the rocks."

A few minutes later he had the drink in his hands. For a while he just looked the place over. There was a small combo playing something that sounded like a cross between rock and roll and hillbilly music. A few dancers. Otherwise the place was empty.

He turned to the barman.

"I was wondering..." he began, and then his voice faded out. The cold stare of the man froze the words in his mouth. He started over. "Could you give me some information?"

52

The man leaned forward. The expression on his face was blank. "Yeah, buddy?"

Robert took a deep breath and said: "I just wanted to know if you knew a certain woman. A Carol Benton. She used to..."

The man shook his head. "Never heard of her."

Robert reached into his jacket and pulled out a wallet. He took out a picture of his wife and handed it to the man. "This is the girl."

The man looked at the picture for a brief moment and shook his head.

"No...don't know her. Never saw her in my life." He handed the picture back and then stepped away to the other end of the bar.

Robert felt a sense of anger. He had fumbled the whole thing. The approach had all been wrong. And for some reason he felt that the man *did* know Carol. He had been too quick to say that he didn't know her. He had been too anxious to deny any knowledge of her.

Maybe he should have offered some money?

He looked down at the drink in his hands, then raised it to his mouth. Downing it, he placed a bill on the bar and walked out.

He wanted to get out of the place. It was a dead end as far as he was concerned.

And, anyway, there wasn't really any reason for him to think that the man knew Carol. It wasn't the type of place that she would hang around—he was sure of that!

Yet something told him that the man had been lying.

Angrily he walked down the street, thinking. There was only one possible contact: *Ruth Kirby.*

There was no doubt in his mind that she had known Carol and that she had been lying. There was only one way that he was going to get any information from her: the direct way. Force if necessary.

Finally he got to his car and slid behind the wheel. He needed time to think. But not too much. Just long enough to get to Ruth Kirby's apartment. From then on he could play it ad-lib.

He started the engine and drove in the direction of the woman's apartment.

His mind kept repeating, almost dully: Carol was *dead.*

But he couldn't feel any emotion.

Oh, there was the seething rage under the controlled surface. But that was totally different from pain and love and anguish and grief. It was as if all those feelings had been drained out of him. As if every emotion had died when Carol had died. All that was left was the desire to kill. That was what he had to do before he ended his own life.

The thought amazed him.

He hadn't realized it before, but there was the sure knowledge that this was exactly what he planned to do. He didn't know exactly when that feeling might have come upon him. But he knew that it had been lurking in his subconscious for days now. Every day since his wife's death.

After Carol's murder had been avenged he would walk off someplace and end his own life.

He pointed the car up the freeway ramp and then into the traffic heading west.

Forty-five minutes later he was parking outside of Ruth Kirby's apartment. He killed the engine and then stepped out of the car.

For a moment he looked in the direction of her apartment windows. There was a light in them. He took a deep breath and let it out between his lips. Then finally he stepped forward.

Then he was knocking on Ruth Kirby's door.

There was the sound of footsteps and then the door opened. Ruth Kirby was standing there, a tight fitting red dress caressing every voluptuous curve of her figure.

For a moment she looked out, and then a gasp sounded from her startled lips. An expression of concern clouded her features.

"Go away," she whispered in a frightened voice. "Get out of here—*quick!*"

For a moment Robert felt the urge to obey her demand, then he shook his head and pushed forward.

There was a hard, muscular man sitting on the sofa, a drink in his hands, He stood, a half sneer clouding his brutal features.

"What the hell do *you* want?" he demanded, angrily.

"None of your business!" Robert snapped back.

"This is Mr. Gordon!" Ruth Kirby cried, stepping in front of Robert.

At first he thought that she was telling him the name of the other man. Then, he realized the truth. *He* was being introduced as Gordon, not the other man. For a moment he started to correct her, then he saw the desperate warning expression in her eyes.

There was something wrong here, and she was trying to warn him about it. Warn him in the only way she knew how. But what was wrong? What *could* be wrong? And why was she trying to warn him? After this afternoon, too?

He decided to play it like she directed—and find out the answers!

CHAPTER SEVEN

There was a moment as the two men looked at each other, and then the man offered him a toothy smiled. "I'm Jake. Jake Turner."

Robert had the feeling that the man could see right through him, reading his thoughts. It was a terrifying feeling, because he didn't have any doubt that this was a man who could be as cold as ice, and as dangerous as a speeding car in the hands of a drunk.

Ruth nervously stepped up to Robert and, taking his arm, said: "He's June's friend. I met him this afternoon. They were visiting. I'll go get June."

She stepped from the room, leaving them alone.

"What do you do?" Jake asked carefully, looking into Robert's eyes.

"I'm not doing anything right now. On a vacation."

"Known June very long?" Jake inquired.

"Long enough." Robert didn't know what kind of a game Ruth was trying to play, but there wasn't any doubt that it was a dangerous and desperate game.

Ruth returned and at her side was June Edmondson. She had on a tight blue sweater and a flaring skirt. She smiled happily and rushed toward

Robert.

"Oh, Bob, I'm so glad that you could make it! I was afraid that you wouldn't show up tonight. After what I said..." She moved to his side and kissed him full on the mouth.

Much to his surprise there was a warm tingling effect from the touch of her lips on his. They were amazingly soft, velvet, warm; very sensual.

She took hold of his arm and squeezed it anxiously. "Well, where are we going?"

"I...?"

"Oh, but who cares? Just being with you is enough. After all these months, it's so good to see you!" June turned to Jake and said: "Bob and I have known each other for years. He's from my home town. You know how it is...haven't seen each other for so long that—you don't mind if we leave you two alone, do you?"

Jake smiled and nodded: "I can't say that I mind at all. Run along, and have fun."

June ushered Robert out before he could say anything. Once outside the apartment, June whispered, "Where's your car? Let's get out of here—*fast!*"

"What the hell!" was Robert's only reaction.

"Don't argue! Your life depends on it!" she told him.

She shoved him lightly forward. Shrugging, he moved in the direction of his car and a few moments later the two of them were driving down the street. Once a couple of blocks had been put between them and the apartment, Robert brought the car to a stop at the side of the road and turned to June.

"Okay, what's this all about!" he said in an angry voice. "I don't like being pushed around."

"Look, I don't know anything about this—any more than you do!" she cried, in alarm. "Don't get mad at me!"

"What?"

"Ruth just came into the kitchen and told me to act like I was an old girl friend of yours from my home town. And get you out of there. She said that it was a matter of life and death!"

Robert thought that one over.

"Ruth does know about Carol, then!" he exclaimed.

"Don't look at me. I don't know anything about it," June told him. Then she smiled and said, "Anyway, I got me a date."

Robert stared at June for a long moment, trying to decide what to do with her. There was only one thought that was hammering in his brain: *Ruth Kirby knew about Carol!* He wanted to go question Ruth and find out what she knew. He had finally hit pay dirt, but there wasn't anything that he could do about it for awhile.

"I guess I do...do owe you something for the acting job you did for me," he said with a sigh, wishing that he could be able to get out of the situation. He didn't like the idea of being trapped for the evening with a woman quite as attractive as June Edmondson. He didn't want anything to do with women—except Ruth Kirby. "What do you want to do? See a show?"

"A dinner—if you don't mind. I haven't eaten."

Robert shrugged and started the car. "You know of any places in town? Some place that's good?"

"Not many. I'm a stranger here myself. I came

to town to get into the movies—but nothing has opened up for me yet."

"Well, we might as well try the first place that looks good."

They found a classy steakhouse. The conversation was light and general. She admitted to having just arrived in town a short time before and glad to have a place to stay. "Ruth seems like a nice lady, willing to help a girl getting started in the business. She has a lot of contacts." That was all she said about that. After martinis and steaks, he suggested that they go back to her apartment.

"Oh, we can't do that. That Mr. Turner will be there until quite late. Ruth wants the two of you...well not socializing, I guess. Don't know why, but.... She's afraid of something."

"You mean?—"

"That we'll have to spend the whole evening together." She was silent for a moment and then suggested brightly: "How about dancing?"

The woman was far from unattractive; in fact very stunningly lovely. Under other circumstances he might have been interested. But in reality his own mind was in a daze, as if clouded over. Emotionally all he felt was the determination to get whomever was responsible for his wife's death. It was insane, what had happened to her. A mystery that didn't make sense. Any more than the mystery of her life here in Hollywood. All he wanted to do was find out everything.

"Come on, Bob," June offered, "We might as well make the most of it."

Robert struggled with the thought for a moment, not wanting to hurt June, and not wanting to go dancing with any woman. But finally he decided there wasn't any way out. They asked the waiter where they might go for dancing and the man said that there was a combo starting at nine, right there.

By nine, both of them had had a couple more martinis, and he had learned a lot about June. She was a small town girl with dreams of being a star—much like Carol had been when he had first known her. And the more that he talked to June the more he found himself being drawn to her. There were so many things about her that were like Carol. Not that they were the same type. Carol had always been a little on the shy side; June was more sure of herself. But there was enough about the both women's backgrounds that caused Robert to feel comfortable with June.

When it was time to dance he didn't even mind too much. June was attractive enough. Not in the same way that Carol was, but she had a figure that would make any man sit up and take notice. And the feel of her against him was surprisingly nice. He felt somewhat guilty about having any reaction to the woman. Yet, an automatic male reaction fed its way down spine. When she moved against him, it drove the desire stronger into place. The woman was aware of her effect on him and she smiled up into his eyes, lips just inches from his.

How easy to kiss her. Under the right circumstance he might have done just that.

That was something that bothered him! He didn't *want* to feel any thing for any women. Yet the silky feel of June Edmondson was something that he found impossible to ignore. The rhythm of her soft body as it responded to every action he made as they glided with the movement of the music, was rather nice, warm, charmingly sensual, without being at all crude or aggressive about it.

And dancing was like being caught up in some magical moment, with a partner who is in that special place with you, alone. They were wrapped up in the sound of the music, which held them captive, not only physically, but emotionally, too. Nothing beyond the two of them and the music existed and it continued to bath over them in wave after wave of powerful seductiveness. The universe had focused down, compressed, into the reality of their bodies dancing together. It was quite an illusion that always ended when the music stopped, and then re-existed as the music started up again. And each time the lingering pleasure of it all had longer lasting effect on his nerves and emotional focus. After a while they were simply together, experience their mutual closeness—and that was all that truly existed as long as the dancing continued. And in some ways, subtly, it extended beyond the music itself. The intimacy of it all had a strangely delicious afterglow that couldn't completely be ignored. It wasn't personal, but rather a kind of role each played out with the other. But what magic it contained. And there was a lingering personal reality to it all. June was a very attractive woman.

Suddenly his mind rebelled at the things that were racing through it. He didn't want to think of women. He didn't want to react. He didn't want to desire. All that he wanted was to find Carol's killer!

Finally the music came to an end and the musicians took a break. Robert led June to their table.

"What time is it getting?" he asked awkwardly,

looking at his watch.

"Oh, it's much too early," June's silky voice told him. He couldn't help noticing a hint of humor shading her words, as if she were laughing at him.

"What's wrong?" she asked, smiling brightly. "You aren't afraid of women, are you?"

He looked sharply at her.

"I don't know what you're talking about," he snapped, reaching for his drink and finishing the martini.

"Nothing. Just forget I said it. Please?"

For a moment he didn't say anything; then finally he forced a smile and said: "Okay, let's forget it. After all, I owe you something for what you've done for a total stranger."

"I...I hope we won't be total strangers for long," she said, looking down at her hands. Then suddenly she returned her gaze in his direction. "I don't mean to...what I mean is that...well, I like you. You don't think that I'm being too bold?"

"Of course not. I like you, too." But his reply was automatic, without any deep feeling being revealed. Yet under it was a sense of feeling, a shimmering undercurrent of desire. June was a woman no man could look at without finding a rather raw desire eating away at the root of his mind and body. It was simple, naked animal lust, automatic.

They sat awkwardly for a long while, looking at each other and not saying anything. Finally he suggested that they leave and go someplace else. "We just can't sit here all evening."

A knowing look welled in June's eyes and she smiled as she stood.

Robert paid the bill and the two of them left.

Once in the car, and driving on the boulevard, he turned on the radio and said: "What you do for kicks?"

It was a moment before June answered him, and when she did there was the note of caution to her voice. "Well, I guess the same as any other girl. You have to understand that when a girl comes to the big city to get into movies...well it's pretty hard. Ruthie is going to help me, she says. Yet...Yet I have the feeling...that...well, that Ruthie is involved with... how can I put it?"

"Gangsters?" Robert blurted out, not having really thought beforehand what he was about to say.

"Oh!"

He saw June's hand go to her mouth and a sigh push past her delicate figures. "Oh...no! I don't think *that!*"

But he had the idea that she wasn't quite sure.

"What you want to do?" he asked, trying to change the subject.

"Anything you like."

"Drive around?"

"Why not? I could show you a little of Hollywood. What little I've seen, at least!" she exclaimed in an overly excited voice, as if she were suddenly glad to get off the subject of Ruth Kirby and onto something else.

During the next two hours they saw Hollywood Boulevard and the Chinese Theater, stopping to see all the hand- and footprints of the Stars. They stopped at the Hollywood Bowl, which was closed for the season, but were able to walk around in the dark.

All the time Robert couldn't get over the feeling

that he was being drawn in some way toward June. There was the violent reaction that he experienced when they accidentally happened to touch, or when she reached out and touched his arm. Then toward the last part of the evening when they were walking through Griffith Park, the night wind lightly caressing their cheeks, they held each other's hands, like school kids on their first date, and talked about themselves.

He told June about Carol and something about his past life, with and without his wife.

"It was pretty strange, all of it happening so fast. When she returned home, well, we were in instant love again."

"That can happen. Some people are just meant to be together, don't you think?"

"Well, we'd known one another since we were kids."

"That's important. We all have that kind of relationship. Something that didn't quite work out and wasn't completed. Letting it hand, incomplete, is terrible. Things have to be ended, resolved and aloud to simply fade into our past. But that can never happen until we've found completion...even then things hang on in our memory."

"Still, when I think about it, all of this happened so fast. And...I never did find out much about her life here in Hollywood. I won't stop until I learn as much as there is to know. And get those responsible—" He broke off, turning away from her. He had to hold back the fury and the sudden choking tears that threatened. A couple of deep breathes and he continued, more in control: "Well, that's my story. Young love rediscovered in a whirlwind. I haven't even digested her return—let along all the rest."

Then he was rambling, telling about his years in the service, some of his experiences in Europe, traveling and seeing some famous places.

She listened and said nothing. But there had been a slight tensing of her fingers in his when he told her about his great affection for Carol and of her sudden murder. And there was the light shading of sadness as he expressed his sense of being lost and not caring much about living.

He said: "It's all a deep wound. And it won't heal just like that."

"Maybe you should leave it to the authorities."

"That's no good."

She started to say something then closed her mouth, just staring up at him.

"I know that it seems silly to tell anybody about all this...but I can't help not caring about anything. Except getting those bastards...and learning the truth!"

She broke in at this point for the first time, saying: "Look, Bob, you can't stop living because your wife died. I don't think that's what she would have wanted. And for God's sake, you shouldn't be trying to take the law into your own hands. That's for the police!"

Irritation pushed through him at this moment. Irritation that he had talked at all to June about Carol. Irritation that he had said anything about his plans to get the murderers.

"Well, that's my business!" he suddenly snapped, dropping her hand and starting off toward where he had parked the car.

He heard her heels clicking on the walkway be-

66

hind him, but he didn't slow down or look around. By the time he had reached the car she had caught up with him.

Her hand reached out and touched his. "I'm sorry. But you told me..."

"Oh, sure! Okay, let's drop it!"

He helped her into the car and he walked around and slid in on the driver's side, starting the engine and directing the car out of the park

June didn't say anything for a long time, then she suddenly blurted out: "You don't really mean what you said, do you?"

"About *what?*"

"About trying to find who killed your wife, and then..."

"Killing them?"

"That's...right." Her voice was deep with concern.

"Why?"

"Because...because you know that's not right. That you can't—"

"Take the law into my own hands!" he growled angrily. "We'll see. We'll just see! Those bastards, who ever they are, have to pay..."

"I know that you can't do it. You aren't a killer!"

"Drop it, will you!" he commanded, gunning the car faster, wanting to get rid of her as soon as possible.

"I...I'm *sorry!*" she said, biting her lower lip and looking away from him.

An hour later he had dropped her off at her apartment and headed toward his hotel. All the way back him to his room he had an disquieting feeling that centered around June Edmondson and his reactions to her, and the fact he had told her so much.

He was a damned fool! he thought when he entered the hotel room and closed the door behind him. He shouldn't have told her about anything—he shouldn't and have told anybody! How'd he know that she wouldn't go to the police?

Yet he had the strange feeling that he could trust June Edmondson; that she was the kind of woman that didn't talk, that didn't tell things that had been told her in private.

But this wasn't the only thing that was bothering him. There was the fact he had talked to her about Carol and himself. He had felt something deep down inside that had drawn him to June in a strangely personal way.

Angrily, he undressed and slipped under the covers, trying to put the matter out of his mind. He had a lot of things to take care of the next day. The first was to see Ruth Kirby. But see her without seeing June Edmondson!

For some reason he was afraid of June and her flaming red hair and desirable body that drew him like a piece of metal to a magnet. He was afraid of the way she made him feel...

Finally sleep forced the tormented thoughts from his tired and bewildered brain, clouding over his conscious awareness and leaving peaceful nothingness.

CHAPTER EIGHT

When June and Robert left the apartment, Ruth Kirby heaved a silent breath of relief, and for a moment she was almost afraid to turn toward Jake Turner; afraid that the expression on her face might give her away. That would be all that she needed after all the quick work that she had managed to pull off!

When she had seen Robert Bradley at the door, panic had shot through her. The first reaction had been to shove him into the hall and not let him in. Then she had realized the foolishness of that action, since it would have been a dead giveaway. The only thing that she had known she wanted to do was to keep Jake from knowing why Bradley was there; and who he was. That was the least thing she could do for the memory of Carol Benton.

Now she had to play it through with Turner. And she was suddenly afraid that she couldn't do it. Jake wasn't a fool; yet there was no reason for him to suspect anything. The fear was all in her mind; that was the trouble with her—she had too many things on her mind. Slowly she tightened her stomach muscles and turned toward Jake.

"Well, I was wondering when you'd remember me!" he said, smiling across the room at her.

69

"I'm sorry, I just got to thinking." Quickly she added: "They make such a nice couple—it's a shame that June can't really get serious with him,"

"Come on, Ruthie. We're in the business of getting her to think about a career in a rather demanding business, where a girl has to be willing to take *any* man to bed with her. Which means she has to be single."

"Oh, it's not that," she exclaimed, taking up the story and hoping that he would believe it; that it would sound logical and real. "It's just that she's...well, she's using the guy. And he's such a nice guy. You know how it is—"

"I know how it is!" Jake laughed. "And it just goes to show you that she's our type of woman!" His expression changed suddenly, and his eyes made a pointed stop at the dip of her dress where her breasts were so revealingly displayed. "Let's forget all this! I see two rather delightful objects far more interesting!"

As usual, the man was bloody obvious.

Ruth felt relief flood through every cell and nerve of her body. Jake had just made it quite possible for her to change the subject and get his mind off Robert and June.

She shivered a little, letting her breasts wiggle invitingly.

"Now, what would you have in mind?" she asked, smiling broadly and moving toward the man.

"Now wouldn't you like to know?" he said, pulling her down to him as she slid into his arms. "Wouldn't you like to know?"

"That's exactly what I mean to find out. I—"
His lips stopped hers. There was a long kiss and

then she felt his fingers dig into her breasts, sliding in under the silky cloth. A murmur of pleasure moved through her

"You're so good!" she sighed in his ear, biting the lobe violently.

He yelled in pain and pulled away.

"Damn it all, that wasn't nice!" he growled, angrily.

"Well, a girl has to eat! Since you aren't taking me out for dinner—I thought I'd start on you!" she laughed, knowing the man liked his sex in a rather violent way, giving and taking.

"What the hell!" he objected. Then the expression on his face changed and he reached out and yanked her brutally against him. He clawed at her back, bruising her lips against his mouth. Then she felt the probing moisture of his tongue as it reached past her teeth. His fingers worked at the back of her dress, then anxiously yanked, all but ripping it off.

A thrill of excitement shot through her as he jerked aside the cloth, savagely pulled down the top of her bra and ripped it off. The fiery expression on his face was a mixture of passion and anger. Once before she had seen him like this, and that had been the first night they had been together. She'd been teasing him and he had suddenly exploded, all but raping her. Much to her surprise it had been the most exciting sexual experience in her life. Now she knew that it was going to be a wild repeat!

He forced her back on the couch and then started working the palms of his hands on her breasts until she wanted to scream! Then suddenly he yanked all the clothing off. Then he pushed down against her, caressing her with his body.

She thought that she'd go out of her mind with the pleasure and pain of it all. Her body responded to his every touch, eagerly.

For a long time they were lost in the hot pleasure of their bodies; aware only of the savagery of their lovemaking. Finally, when it was over, he stood and dressed.

"Come on—let's go get something to eat!" he demanded.

* * * * * * *

June stepped into the apartment to find it empty. Sighing, she moved across the living room, trying to get the deep depression from her mind when she thought about Robert Bradley. She liked the man, and strangely found herself drawn to him in such a powerful way that she felt as if she had known him for years. That could happen between strangers. They met and almost instinctively were drawn to one another. She had felt his interest in her, though it was continually clouded over, as if he were fighting it down. Obviously it was too soon after his wife's death to be seeking another relationship. Maybe he never would want such intimacy. The pain was obvious.

Yet, June knew that if they had met under other circumstances they may have actually even ended up in his hotel room, spending the rest of the night in one another's arms; the first of many such nights.

Slowly she got undressed and slipped into a pink nightie. Looking at herself in the mirror she couldn't help thinking that Robert would like to see her now!

72

Under the right circumstances.

After all, he was a man. And she had no doubts about her own attractiveness to men. All through her teenage life she'd been popular with the guys at school. They all wanted to date her. She never was without a date. And that popularity had feed into the desire to become an actress.

Looking at herself, now, she felt quite proud of how good she looked.

The sheer netting showed every lovely curve of her figure, almost revealing the pink centers of her breasts. Men were always all-day suckers for a woman's beasts. She smiled, thinking that she would *like* to have Robert Bradley see her like that!

Robert Bradley, a man that it would be easy to fall for; a man who had a driving urge to destroy himself and gain revenge on the people who had killed his wife. How sad, all of that. And terribly frightening.

It wasn't hard to understand such feelings. Yet she had a strong desire to stop him, somehow, to re-direct his pain and fury to safer grounds. Let the police deal with it. She'd been right about that.

The idea of this lovely man ruining his future over something he could not change in his past, seemed such a waste.

If only they had met under different circum-stances.

Maybe she was simply lonely for a man.

She tried to think about other things, because suddenly her thoughts about Robert Bradley were beginning to bother her, and the last thing she wanted was to get emotionally involved with an-other person and their problems. She had enough of her own!

Sighing, she stepped toward her bed and started slipping under the covers when she heard the front door open and Ruth call out.

"Are you there?" the other woman's voice questioned. "June?"

"Yes, Ruthie."

Ruth Kirby stepped into the bedroom and turned on the light. "I have a few things to talk to you about."

The woman paused for a moment and then, after walking over to the bed and sitting down, said: "But first I have a few things I want to ask you."

June saw it coming and wished that there were some way of getting out of the conversation. But reluctantly she sat up and looked at the other woman.

"Go ahead," she sighed.

"About this Mr. Bradley."

"I thought so."

"What'd you find out?"

"He's a nice man."

Ruth looked at her for a moment, her brow wrinkling in thought, then she asked: "What'd you find out about—"

"Why he wants to know about Carol, his wife?'

"That's right."

"She was murdered."

"He told me that today."

"And he wants to find the murderer."

"That much I knew. I want to know the details. It's important. His life might depend on it!"

"Oh, look, Ruthie. I'm not a spy or something. I said that I like the guy and he told me a lot of things that he shouldn't have told me—in private. I don't think that he wants me to blab it all around."

"Now look here!" Ruth snapped angrily. "You don't know what you're talking about. The people that he's after—or the people I *think* he's after are deadly! He doesn't know what he's getting into. If he puts his nose in the wrong door asking questions, he'll be found in the ocean—dead!"

For a moment June looked at Ruth, not saying anything. Her fear that she had been getting involved with the wrong group of people suddenly welled up and she couldn't think of what to say. She was almost afraid to say anything! Then finally she decided that the best plan was to play along. She was already involved, and there wasn't any backing out now. She'd come to Hollywood to become a big star. Her destiny had been set into action, and she couldn't move from that path even if she wanted to. June suddenly knew that, and the realization left her momentarily numb. And confused.

"Robert Bradley came to Hollywood to find and kill the person or persons responsible for his wife's death. He doesn't care anything about his own life or safety. Right now the only thing that seems to matter to him is killing...nothing else. I don't think he's the kind of man who could kill." June's voice was heavy and thick, but without any emotion.

"You'd be surprised what some men can do. But maybe you're right. Maybe not."

June tried to shrug that off. "I just think he has a lot of pain."

She had made her report, and that was the end of it; and she couldn't help thinking that it was also the end of something inside her that had had a sense of values. But she pushed aside the thought. Willed it out of her mind.

"Is that all? All you need to know?" she asked.

Ruth sat thinking, not aware that June had spoken. Finally she shook her head from side to side. "That poor damned fool. That damned fool!"

Slowly she stood and walked out of the room.

June lay in bed, trying to make her mind blank and not think about Robert Bradley. But she found her thoughts constantly returning to him. Then finally sleep overcame her tired mind and body.

She dreamed of Robert.

The two of them were on a lonely beach. She had on a very brief bathing suit that showed off every curve of her body. And Robert kept looking at her as if he couldn't look hard enough.

Suddenly his hand reached out and pulled the top piece of her bathing suit off.

"Such lovelies, they are!" he murmured, eyes feasting on her breasts.

She laughed at him. "You men, all you want to do is look at boom city! What's the fascination on a woman's breasts. It is such a laugh!"

"Cause they're so beautiful and ripe and full and round and—"

"Wanna suckie, suck on mommy's titties? Like a little baby?"

"Come here, you woman," he said in a heated voice. "I think you owe me something for what you told Ruth Kirby—and now I'm going to take full payment!"

Then the two of them were rolling on the sand, until she wanted to scream out in the ecstasy of it all! His lips crushed hers, open and probing. She felt his tongue reach past her teeth.

His hands fondled her breasts and then she felt the stabbing pain as his nails dug deeply into her. A convulsive excitement rippled through every nerve of her body as he forced himself harder against her, and then suddenly their bodies blended, blurred and suddenly everything was numb.

Her eyes opened and focused on the ceiling of her bedroom. She felt a stab of shock at her dream and the words she had used in it. Her dream-self was so totally opposite her real self. That was more shocking than anything else. Then slowly it all kind of faded, and became somewhat comical.

The sun was bright in her eyes, almost blinding her. It was morning.

June lay there, trying to figure out why she had had such a vividly passionate dream. And so distorted. But she found no answer, except a desire to be with Robert Bradley again.

That was the only truth it contained.

And that thought bothered her the rest of the morning. The next time she saw Robert Bradley she was going to do everything she could to make him interested in her! Somehow. It was a foolish, desperate play; but maybe if she was able to seduce him in a sexual way, pure erotic escape, she could turn his mind away from the obsession for revenge. A revenge that he could hardly bring about. And which could, very possibly, kill him.

She realized that she wanted his body; she wanted to feel her arms around him; she wanted to have him make love to her! And that was real, too.

And as totally insane as that might be, it was there, alive deep within her. And it didn't make any sense. Nor did her wild thought that a sexual union could turn his mind away from the mission that had brought him to Hollywood. Not a chance. Any more than there was a chance she could turn off her ambitions that had brought her to this town.

CHAPTER NINE

When Robert Bradley woke up the next morning he suddenly found himself facing several conclusions.

One: he wasn't really getting anywhere. He *had* found out that Ruth Kirby had known Carol, and that she no doubt knew something about Carol's life in Hollywood. But he'd allowed himself to be pushed around; forced into a date with June Edmondson.

Two: he had to find a way of questioning Ruth Kirby. That was the next logical step. But what if she didn't *want* to tell him anything? What if she refused to tell him anything at all?

Three: it was going to take more time than he had thought. At first he had believed that it would simply be a matter of finding the contacts and then rushing forward. Now he realized it was going to take some serious time. One thing he did know was that Carol hadn't been killed with just a single bullet; she had been riddled with a score or so from a sub-machine gun. That meant gangsters. And gangsters meant organization. And organization meant great danger. There was a viciousness about the killing. Usually, one imagined, a bullet to the back of the head would be good enough. This had been done as if trying to make an example, to make a statement. But to whom? For whom? Why?

Maybe he was crazy trying to go up against them. Maybe he should hire a detective. Or go to the police like June had suggested.

For some reason he felt those actions would get him nowhere. Police could be bought off. He was a stranger in the town. Who could he trust?

Robert's mind was seething in confusion. It hadn't been working solidly since the tragic night Carol had been killed. Only in rage had he experienced any deep focus. He'd keep his mind on that, again focusing on nothing else.

He had gotten so far by that sheer blind passion. Now he suddenly became consciously aware of what he was attempting to do, and an inner cord of caution made him stop and think.

Maybe this sudden change of attitude had something to do with June Edmondson.

He forced that from his mind, not wanting to even think about the woman—any woman. He had only one point to make, and that was to find Carol's killers!

He lay in bed thinking for a long time and then finally got up and dressed, had breakfast and called Ruth Kirby's number.

The phone was answered by June Edmondson.

"Hello, Miss Edmondson," he said in a formal voice, wanting to make a direct point that he didn't want anything to get started between them.

"Who is this?" her light voice asked.

"Mr. Bradley."

"Oh, Bob, how nice to hear from you so—"

"Is Miss Kirby there?" he asked in an impersonal tone.

"No—she's down at the office."

"Where's that?"

There was a pause on the other end and then finally June told his that the other woman worked for a business investment firm. She gave him the number and he hung up, dialed and waited.

"Can I speak to Miss Ruth Kirby?" he asked the operator.

A moment later he heard Ruth's voice over the receiver. "Hello, this is Robert Bradley—I was wondering if I could have lunch with you…for last night. I feel I owe you something."

He had hardly finished when she said to meet her at the Brown Derby at twelve-thirty, then she hung up.

Checking his watch, Robert discovered that he had less than forty-five minutes before his sudden luncheon engagement. A sense of excitement was rushing through him all at once. For the first time since he'd gotten to Hollywood, it looked like he was beginning to get somewhere! Yet there was a strange disquieting feeling; a sense of walking into something that might lead into a blind alley. Or a dangerous trap. Maybe it was because of Ruth Kirby's attitude about seeing him; as if she had been *waiting* for him to contact her.

Shrugging, he walked from his room to the hotel lobby and asked the desk clerk where he could find the Brown Derby.

"Just a few blocks east. You can't miss it. Vine Street—south of Hollywood Boulevard," the man directed him.

It took him less than five minutes to walk to the

famous restaurant. There were still more than thirty minutes before Ruth Kirby would arrive, so he walked to the cocktail lounge and ordered a martini. He was sipping on his second when Miss Kirby walked into the lounge and stepped over to where he was sitting. There was a bright smile on her face; but it had the look of being slightly forced.

"Hello, how are you today?" he asked, conversationally. But there was an edge to her voice, an edge of warning. She leaned closer and whispered: "Be careful. I don't know, but I think I've been followed. I'll tell you later all about it. Come on out with me. I have a car. We can talk then."

A few minutes later they were in her car driving along Hollywood Boulevard. Neither of them said anything for a long while and then it was Ruth who started the conversation.

"What do you want to find out about Carol Benton?"

"I told you: she was murdered. I need to know about her life...here. And the people she knew."

There was a pause before Ruth said anything. Then she took a deep sigh and cried: "Drop it! If you have any sense, just drop it!"

"I can't!" he countered, looking sharply at her. "And I don't think that it's any of your business to be concerned about."

Ruth turned and said: "Maybe a little hard reality will shock you into being smart. Look, you don't know what you're getting into. Last night if Jake Turner had known who you were and what you wanted, you would have been dead this morning!"

Robert tensed, as if jolted by an electric shock.

"That's right." she continued. "He's a trigger

man for a rather widespread syndicate. He makes a lot of people jump—and they jump because they are afraid of him!" She stopped suddenly, biting her lower lip. "I really don't know why I'm telling you this. Maybe because I like you—because of Carol. Well...it doesn't matter. The thing I want to get through your stupid head is that you aren't playing around with the *little* boys. This is upstairs, where the big boys play, and they play damn rough! And dirty. And for keeps!"

"I'm not worried about that."

"Why don't you just drop it before you get into matters that are beyond...just take my word for it. Carol ran away. She knew when to quit!"

"What do you mean by that?" Robert asked, startled by her statement.

"You don't know what she did here in Hollywood? What she was?" Ruth countered, glancing over toward him for a moment. Her face had the look of surprise.

"That's what this whole thing is about. If I knew anything about her activities here in town I would have known exactly where to go."

Ruth didn't say anything for a long while, driving in silence. Then suddenly she pulled the car toward the curb and parked it, cutting off the engine. Slowly she turned to Robert, a tense expression on her face. "Won't you just forget this whole thing?"

"It's not that simple."

"Go back home. Forget about what happened here. What happened to your wife. That she's been murdered."

"I'm sorry, that's quite impossible. I don't know what you must think of me. But get this one point straight. I loved my wife and she was killed. And there's another point. We were going to have a baby. The people who are responsible for her death were also responsible for killing our child!"

Ruth bit her lower lip nervously, looking away from him for a moment. Then taking a deep breath she said: "If you don't forget this...you're going to be dead. That's the truth of it. And you don't deserve dying. But much worse for you will be what you'll find out about your dear wife." Her voice was a mixture of bitterness and sarcasm. "And you really don't want to know that. Believe me!"

"What are you talking about?"

"Simply that..." Ruth paused and then seemed to decide something. "Do you really want to know about Carol Benton? Do you really want to know what she became during her ten years in this city?"

"That's what I came here to find out."

"Okay, you asked for it. If this doesn't blow your mind, then nothing will. If this doesn't convince you to drop it all, forever, nothing will. Sometimes hard, harsh, cruel reality can do what kindness never can. But don't blame me. There's only one way to make you think realistically about this. And if it weren't for Carol I'd let you go to hell and back." She stopped for a moment and then continued, looking Robert directly in the eyes. "Your wife came to Hollywood to become a Big Star in the movies. Instead she became a Big Hollywood Party Girl. And if you don't know what that means I'll explain it for you in simple terms: she was a call-girl. A woman who sold her body to men for anything from $250 a night to $1,500 a night. And up!"

Robert just sat there stunned, unable to think,

unable to feel anything. The statement left him numb.

"But, that's not all! She was, at the last, a mistress for a big time rackets man here in town. When she finally got fed up, she tried getting out. She went home to you—but she knew too much and the big boys were afraid of what she might someday tell the authorities, so they took the simple way out and had her killed."

Ruth started to say something else, but Robert didn't stay to listen. He didn't want to hear any more! He'd been told that his wife was the lowest type of female tramp. Then that she'd been the mistress to a hood. It was either some fantastic lie or...

He was going mad!

Robert didn't remember getting out of Ruth's car or slamming the door or walking away along the street. He didn't remember going into a bar and ordering one martini after another. His mind had taken one shock after another and this last one created a complete blackout. The next thing he knew was that he was lying on a bunk, hard and cold, in the city jail.

* * * * * * *

When Robert Bradley walked suddenly out of her car, Ruth just sat, staring straight ahead for a long time. Then finally she sighed and started the engine. She had to get back to work. She wasn't hungry. There was something inside her that was dead, and the only way she could reason that out was because of what she had had to tell Bradley. She didn't like herself for having done it, but there just hadn't been anything else that she could do. It had been her only hope to get him off his trail toward death. And that was where he would land! That much she knew. Jake Turner would kill him as quickly as he would swat a fly!

She didn't want to see that happen, if for no other reason than the fact that she held a deep affection toward the memory of Carol, a girl who had tried to get out of a nasty trap from which there just wasn't any escape, *except death!*

The rest of the afternoon was a slowly moving hell for Ruth, but she managed to keep busy.

Then finally six came—and also Jake Turner!

When they were in *Rolly's Inn,* and had finished their first drink and were working on the second, she looked across at Turner, trying to think how she was going to question him about Carol Benton. She *had* to find out how the woman had been killed.

"Say, I was wondering," she began, trying to sound only curious, "what ever happened to Carol Benton?"

Jake jerked at the name.

"Why do you ask?" His eyes narrowed and he looked carefully at her.

"Well, I've heard stories about her having been killed." She hadn't meant to say that; the words had blurted out.

For a long time the man didn't say anything. "Well, you know how it is. She walked out on Dave. And he doesn't go for that."

"You were the one that gave the order?" she asked, hiding the bitterness from her voice.

"What's gotten into you?" Jake demanded. His voice had the edge of suspicion. "What business is it of yours?"

"Oh—nothing. I was just wondering. I'd heard these stories, and knowing that you are the man who—"

"Well, forget it! Or you'll end up like she did! There are reasons for certain things happening. She knew too much, and we couldn't take the chance of her blabbing all around." He paused, and then said: "What brought it up?"

"I don't know what you mean."

"I mean exactly that! What brought it up?"

"Oh, nothing. Nothing at all. Just the stories. That's all."

Neither of them said anything for a long time, then Jake suddenly changed the subject. But there was something in his manner; the way he talked, that gave her the idea that he hadn't *really* finished with the subject!

CHAPTER TEN

When Robert woke and found himself in jail, his first reaction was not to do anything about it. Nothing mattered to him. He just didn't care what happened to him, or how he had gotten there. There was only one emotion left in him: a sense of complete and utter defeat. For some reason he could now accept what he hadn't wanted to the day before:

His wife a prostitute. A gangster's mistress!

Strangely, it all seemed to fit. It was a logical reason why she had never told him anything about her life in Hollywood; the reason that those ten years had been kept a complete mystery.

But what hurt him most was not knowing *why* she had turned to such a life of sin; why she had become what Ruth Kirby had said she was.

Carol—a call girl!

It took several hours for him to realize that it really didn't matter. That no matter what she'd become, she hadn't deserved to die. To realize that the good side of her *had* been honest. And then a new determination surged through him. A desire to finish what he had started!

He knew that Carol must have gone through a series of events that had pushed her through a knothole, backwards. Carol just wasn't the type of woman who would become a prostitute by choice! Circumstances must have gotten out of control, and she must have found herself being sucked down a whirlpool over which she had no control. He suddenly realized that Ruth Kirby hadn't told him everything. She hadn't told the complete truth!

But where did that leave him?

In jail.

Now he wanted out. He wanted to fight back again!

It didn't take long to get a police guard and then finally find out when he would be let out. He was supposed to appear before a judge that afternoon and be fined for being drunk and disorderly. By four in the afternoon he would be out of jail.

* * * * * * *

June Edmondson was ironing when Ruth Kirby came home. Ruth had been away all night, and there was an inner sense of anxiety in June.

Ruth looked tired and nervous, but she didn't say anything for a long time. Then finally it was June who asked: "What are you doing home so early?"

"I didn't go to work. That's why!" Ruth snapped back.

"Well, you don't have to get mad!"

"I'm sorry, June, but I have a few things on my mind." For a moment Ruth paused in the middle of the room, looking at June, but not saying anything. Then finally she seemed to make up her mind. "You know that Mr. Bradley I had you go out—"

"Oh, you mean Bob? Of course. What about

89

him?"

"Well—I was talking to Jake Turner." She broke off, abruptly.

"Well? Go on," June encouraged. She wanted to know what Ruth had to say; she had the feeling that it was important to Robert Bradley, and she wanted to help the man; she wanted to find some way to help him find himself. *Find himself for her.* That thought made her numb with surprise. She hadn't realized that she actually felt so strongly toward him. It was one thing to be attracted to a man; quite another to go out and try to win him, get him.

"We...we have to warn him. We have to help him—some way." Ruth tensed suddenly. "But I don't even know where he lives."

"What are you talking about?"

"He's got to be stopped, before...before it's too late."

"You're kidding!"

"No—these people play rough!" Ruth paused, cutting her words short, as if she realized that she had said too much. "Well, you've heard that much," she finally said, "So you might as well hear the rest." There was a moment of silence, then Ruth continued: "Carol Benton came to Hollywood to get into the movies. She got into the...wrong group. Finally she was the girl friend of an important man in the Syndicate. When she tried to get out—well, they saw to it that she was silenced...murdered."

There was a heavy quiet after that. Then after a while, Ruth said: "We have to get Robert Bradley off their trail. If they find out what he is trying to do—he'll be killed without any warning. These people don't care anything about human lives..." Ruth's voice caught, a choking sob stopping her words. "What am I doing? Why am I telling you?"

June didn't have anything to say about that, she just sat there trying to think things out. She realized exactly what the other woman's words implied. The people that Ruth was involved with were dangerous; they were the *wrong* kind of people to get connected with. And now she had gotten involved with June.

Suddenly fear moved through her; fear that it might be too late to get out; too late to save her own life—to find any kind of happiness in a safe line of business! She was beginning to wonder if becoming a Hollywood star was so important; becoming a great actress for any reason seemed suddenly shallow. There certainly were other things in life—the kind of life her parents had lived. A married life, raising kids, having a family, had always seemed so mundane and such a waste. Now she wondered. Maybe the normal, run-of-the-mill kind of existence wasn't all that bad. She was confused, uncertain. There had to be some middle ground between those extremes. With somebody like Bob it might not be that difficult. Of course, he was totally involved with his own tragic experiences. And that was leading to a quick grave, if he didn't watch out.

June felt deep frustration and uncertainty. It was difficult to sit there talking to Ruth without revealing her own true feelings—and those she wasn't quite sure of, for they involved things which were totally alien to what had driven her to Hollywood in the first place.

She asked: "What can we do?"

Ruth sighed, shrugging her shoulders. "That's just the point. There really *isn't* anything that we can do. Nothing that I can think of. The trouble with Robert Bradley is that he just doesn't care about his life—I only hope that I knocked the guts out of him yesterday. I told him what his wife had been. And he reacted the way I hoped he would. Yet I have the feeling that it didn't stop him. That he would get over it and want revenge anyway."

"What can we do?" June asked again, feeling a sickness inside.

"Honey, the only thing that we can really do is to do nothing! There just isn't anything that can be done. We can try just once more—if he comes around we can do our best to get him to return home and forget the whole thing. That's all." But from the worried expression on Ruth's face, June had the idea that there was *something else* they could do!

* * * * * * *

Robert Bradley got into his car and drove toward Ruth Kirby's apartment. He had to find out more information about Carol! Find out names and places. From there, it would be up to him to follow through. But he had to find out who had killed Carol—who was responsible. Then he would worry about what to do about it. First things had to come first.

When he stood before the apartment door he had the feeling that he was stepping toward the line from which there would be no return! Everything that had happened up to this point had been blind fury—now it was being done with full knowledge of what he was getting into.

He paused for a second and then rang the door

bell. A second later it opened and June Edmondson looked out.

A look of surprise and relief flashed across the woman's features.

"Oh, God, am I glad to see you!" she choked out, excitedly. "Come on in—*quick!*"

Robert moved into the room, and June slammed the door behind him.

"Is Ruth Kirby here?" he asked.

"No—not right now. She just left a few minutes ago. Jake Turner called and she went over to his place."

Robert felt a sense of defeat. "When will she be back?"

"I don't know—but...you have to get out of here. You have to get away. Fast, before *they* kill you!"

"Who kills me?"

"Tur—I don't know. Ruth said..."

"Turner? Is that who you mean?"

"Did I say that? How would I know? I don't know anything! Nothing at all! Just do as I told you!"

Robert didn't wait for another word to be exchanged, but instead walked over to where he saw a phone was in the corner. If there were a phone book there, there might be a phone and address book.

It was there.

He picked it up and flipped it to "Turner."

"You can't do that!" June cried, rushing over and trying to take it from him

Forcefully he pulled the girl away. "Just don't push me, June. I don't want to hurt you."

He found the name Jake Turner and an address listed in Beverly Hills. Turning he moved across the room toward the door, with the book still tightly graphed in his hand. A moment later he was in the hallway. Shortly after that he was getting into his car and starting the engine. Just as he was about to pull away from the curve June opened the door on the passenger side and slid in, closing the door after her.

"What the hell are you doing—?"

"I'm coming with you!" she said firmly.

"It's none of your business!" he snapped, angrily.

"I'm making it mine," she countered, her voice tight with stubborn conviction.

Robert took one look at her and then gunned the car. He didn't care about her or what happened to her or anybody. All he cared about was taking the next step to revenge. Regardless of what happened. Why she wanted to come along, or what might happen to her, didn't concern him in the least. It was almost as if she wasn't there.

CHAPTER ELEVEN

As Robert Bradley drove through Hollywood, he couldn't get his mind off the girl sitting in the car next to him. He was thinking about that other time, a couple of nights ago, when he had been *forced* out on a date with her. Now he wondered just exactly what had caused him to take her out. Not fear. Maybe confusion. But whatever it was, he had the sickening feeling that it involved some inner attractiveness about June Edmondson that he didn't want to consciously admit.

June was an attractive woman; a woman that a man would be more than pleased to be seen out with; a woman that a man would be more than thrilled to take to bed. She had a body that not only attracted the eye, but also the guts.

He didn't dare speak to her; he didn't dare even recognize the fact to her that he thought she existed. There was something about the girl's manner that warned that she had more than casual interest in him—what that could be after only two meetings, he wasn't able to admit even to himself.

He tried to shrug off her being there. He tried to focus on something else to think about.

He had problems. Plenty of them. And he was heading straight toward the number one: Jake

Turner.

Finally he arrived in the general territory where Jake Turner was supposed to live. Driving into a gas station he asked the attendant the exact location of the address. After being given detailed instructions he started off again. In a few moments he was parking in front of a large hotel.

"I don't know why you came along, but you stay here!" Robert said forcefully to June, as he stepped out of his side of the car. "I don't know what's going to happen..."

"Wait!" June said, desperately. "I have an idea. I've been trying to think of something—and I have an idea!"

He paused for a moment and then said: "What?"

"Listen. Mr. Turner knows you as Gordon—a boy friend of mine. You can get into his apartment that way. Play along with the gag. I'll just say that Ruth had...well we'll play it ad-lib and Ruth will play along. It will be safer and you'll be able to find out what you want in some way—without taking any chances."

He thought that over for a moment and then sighed: "Okay."

The two of them moved across the street and into the large modern hotel. After locating the elevator they went up to the fifth floor and then a little later found the suite numbered 5-7.

For only a moment Robert hesitate and then he rang the door bell on the top of the name plate.

He waited for several seconds and then rang again. And waited. Silence was his only answer. Ringing once more and waiting a little longer he turned to June. "Do you have any idea where they might be?"

June just moved her head from side to side, silently.

"Well then, we'll just have to wait around for awhile. That's about all. Just wait around for a little while."

"Where?" June asked, looking up and down the hall. "We can't wait here."

Robert thought for a moment and then decided. "How'd you like a cocktail?"

"Well, Mr. Robert Bradley, that's a great idea!" June exclaimed.

* * * * * * *

Ruth looked across the desk at Jake Turner and felt an inner nervousness grind through her. She had a good idea why she was here and she didn't like it. There hadn't been a word said, as yet, but she expected the worst, from the expression on Jake's serious face. His eyes were narrowed in deep thought as he settled down in the chair. For a long time he just sat there looking through her, then finally his eyes slowly began to come into focus on her.

"I don't know quite how to bring this up," he said in a tight voice. "If it was anybody other than you, it would be much easier. But business is business and you know the score as well as I do." He took a deep breath and then let it out in a loud sigh. His features tightened and became hard. His mouth a thin line, without any humor. His eyes narrowed down even more, until she could hardy see them. "You've been holding out on me, Ruth—and you know what that means." He paused for a moment, then continued. "There are certain obligations that go with doing business with us. Certain responsibilities—and if they aren't lived up to...then there are certain actions that take place. You might even go as far as to say that there are rules—laws—that must be followed, and if they aren't, then there are punishments for breaking them. A minor offense gets a minor punishment. A major mistake ends you up in the ocean. *Got me?*" His eyes opened wider and his fist pounded on the table top.

"I don't know what you are talking about!" Ruth objected, trying to make her voice sound puzzled; but she had the sick feeling what he was leading up to.

"I think you know. And that's what has got me troubled. I thought that I knew you. I believed that I could trust you, Ruthie—but now I have evidence that makes me think otherwise. And that not only hurts you, but it can cause trouble for me with the Syndicate. Unless I take action. Do you understand what I'm talking about?"

Ruth didn't say anything; she just sat there looking as blankly as she could; trying to keep an even mask on her features so that he couldn't see the terror and confusion and fear that was threatening to reveal itself.

"What I'm trying to make clear to you is that what I'm forced to go through right now isn't easy for me—because there is a certain amount of affection that I feel for you. But let's admit the truth—women are a dime a dozen."

"Why don't you stop fencing and come to the point, Jake?" Ruth demanded tightly,

"Okay, then, to the point, I'll give you one chance about this," He paused and then leaned forward. "Why did you ask about Carol Benton?"

That was the question she'd been afraid of! It had been a mistake to ask about the woman, but something inside her had moved the question out before she had had time to think. It had been a dangerous mistake, because Jake Turner was anything but a fool. The man was able to put two and two together and get some very interesting questions that he would take the time and effort to answer to his satisfaction.

"Well, Jake is that all this is about?' she asked. "God, you had me worried, I thought that you discovered the truth about me working for the FBI or something."

"Don't be funny, Miss Kirby!" Jake snapped.

"Oh, come on, Jake. Don't be silly. I was just wondering about it. You know, you meet a person and have a lot of social activities with them and become friends—and then you hear that they are dead...well you get to wondering, and want to know what happened and—"

"*And stop!* I got to thinking about your question. Why did Ruth ask it? She wouldn't be just asking because she was curious. She wouldn't nose into such matters, because she knows that they aren't her concern. She knows *when* to ask questions, what areas are open and which are closed. *Murder is closed.* Carol Benton is a closed issue. Not to be talked about. So why did Ruth ask? There had to be a good reason. So I did a little checking. First we knew that she had married some slob named Robert Bradley, a boyfriend of hers. So we did a little

99

checking and found that Bradley had been in the hospital in a state of shock one day and then suddenly disappeared. Completely disappeared from Boise: his car and everything. There was a bank draft made in Reno for several hundred dollars. A little checking and we discovered that he was heading in this direction, Hollywood. Now putting two and two together I get some interesting conclusions.

"Bradley is in town. He is looking for the people who killed his wife. He has contacted you. *And for some reason you have decided that you are either helping him or remaining silent!*" He pointed a finger at Ruth. "Am I right?"

Ruth didn't say anything, but she had the terrible feeling that her face gave her away. Thoughts were rushing through her mind. But finally she decided she had to level.

"Okay, Jake, I'll tell you the whole story. He's here in town. He wants the killer of his wife. He doesn't care anything about his own life. The reason that I didn't tell you was because I hoped I could turn him away. I liked Carol Benton—she was a nice girl—and for her sake I tried to save the man she loved. It's as simple as that."

Jake didn't say anything for a moment and then he sighed, relaxing. "Okay, I'll take your word for it that far. But only on one condition. Tell me one thing, first: have you talked him out of nosing around?"

Ruth shook her head from side to side, feeling sick and bitter inside; hating the fear and terror that had forced her to tell Jake the truth.

"Okay then. I'll have to take action!"

"Oh, Jake—*don't!* Give the guy a break. He's a

100

nice guy—you have to understand...his wife was going to have a baby!"

An odd expression clouded Jakes features. "I'm terribly sorry about that—really. But it wouldn't have changed what we had to do."

"But can't you give *him* a break?"

"Oh, come off it, Ruth. Be realistic. We don't kill everybody who gets in our way just for the fun of it. We don't kill unless it is completely necessary. What do you take me for? I'm a human being, too. I'll do everything in my power to help this Mr. Bradley to survive and forget all about his 'mission' here. But we have to take direct action. We don't want to get another killing on the record—it's too dangerous. But if it is necessary, that is exactly what we'll do! There are several lines of action to take. The first is the most direct. You're going to have to help. Set him up for a trap. One way to scare him off is to let him realize two things. One: that he's up against forces that are just too big for him. Two: teach him that he *does* care for his life by almost taking it away from him."

"What do you plan to do?" Ruth sighed out in terror.

"Beat the holy crap out of him. Beat him within an inch of his life. And if that doesn't help...well, we'll have to take final measures."

Ruth felt trapped; she suddenly realized there wasn't anything she could do to stop what was going to take place. She had her own safety to look out for; and she realized that the only way Robert Bradley might he turned away was by setting him up like Jake demanded.

"Well, Ruthie, are you with me or against me?" Jake asked.

"I'm with you. I'll do whatever you want!"

CHAPTER TWELVE

They were sipping their second martini before Robert had calmed down and begun to reason in a rational way. He looked across at June, examining her wide forehead and delicate nose, full lips and large eyes. There was something in her eyes that attracted his attention for a long while. They weren't really innocent; there was a deep understanding about life in them, as if she had already seen something that had taught her it wasn't just a child's game.

"You know that I don't...well you haven't got around to telling me much about yourself," he said, suddenly interested in learning about June.

"There really isn't much to tell, Bob. You know I came from the small town to the big city to see the fame and money that comes to those who get their names in big lights. In a word: I wanted to become an actress and if lucky a big star. The only thing I've seen so far is other people with money and power." There was a sadness in her voice and a faraway look in her eyes. "My father died when I was about ten, my mother just a little before I came to Hollywood. I didn't have anything to hold me. An agent had contacted me at college when he saw me in a play there, and when I got here I looked him up. He was a friend of Jake Turner's. Turner is a friend of Ruth's, and you know the rest."

Robert fingered the rim of his glass, thinking. Thinking about Carol, Ruth and June. They were all the same group. Women who wanted show business. Women that got in the wrong group and found themselves trapped.

"You don't know where Ruth was going?" he asked, trying to get his mind off his thoughts about June.

"No, really. I have no idea. All we can do is wait, I guess. Unless you change your mind." Her voice was thoughtful for a moment. "Are you sure that it's worth it?"

"What?"

"Finding your wife's killers. And then...then *killing.*"

"It's worth it." He took a swallow of the martini and then put down the almost empty cocktail glass. "But I don't really know what I'm going to do when I find them. My thoughts haven't gone that far." Suddenly he realized that he really hadn't made any solid plans. He had moved ad-lib; wanting answers to questions and figuring that he would let matters work themselves out—*maybe that was a mistake.*

He looked up at June and his eyes caught the full pouted cushions of her lips. They were very kissable lips; lips that any man would like to caress with his own.

Angrily, he downed the last of the martini and looked toward the bar. After a little while he caught the eye of the bartender. "Two more!" he said, pointing to the cocktail glasses.

After a moment's silence. June interrupted his

thoughts. "What are you going to do when you find the answers to your questions?"

"I guess kill the man. The only thing I can do."

"What about the police?"

"How could I prove it?" He spread his hands helplessly. "Anyway, what do you care?"

June's features frowned for a moment, then she said: "To be truthful, I don't know." The words came out slowly with a deep amount of thoughtfulness behind them. "I...there's something about you that—" She broke off, her face flushing slightly. "To be honest, Bob, I like you."

It was Robert's turn to flush. But his eyes didn't drop from hers for a long while. "It's no good—you know"

"What difference does it make? I'm here, now—and we can't keep demanding answers for things. Honestly, Bob—maybe 1 shouldn't say this—but I want to help you. I don't know really why. But I want to see that you don't get harmed—" She broke off suddenly and then quickly continued. "I don't know if I *should* care. I don't see why I'm here. And I don't care. There's something that's moving me—and that's that!"

The martinis came and Robert paid for them and then took a large swallow of his. The drinks weren't effecting him and he wanted to feel their effects. He needed something to help focus his mind. Nervously he looked at his watch. It was only half past nine. They'd only been there for a little over an hour. Too soon to check on Turner. He felt a sense of helplessness. Something was always holding him back; keeping him away from moving forward. Maybe it was something within himself. He'd botched up a couple of chances, and now that he wanted to move forward there wasn't anything that he could do but wait.

Suddenly he felt the effects of the martinis as he took another large swallow. It hit his stomach like a bomb, exploding and bouncing up against his brain. Again he looked toward June and saw an expression of deep tenderness. For a moment he didn't quite know how to react to it, then decided to ignore it.

There was something about June that gave him the feeling of unrest; something about his reactions toward her. Nervously he finished his martini, and it ebbed through him like an electric charge affecting his body in a way that was startling.

Suddenly he was more and more aware of the sensual attractiveness of the woman sitting there next to him. Her large, caress able breasts, full and supple. Desirable.

God, the bloody drinks were banging his brain! Maybe natural for a man to react to a woman like this. But he didn't want to.

"Let's get out of here!" he suddenly exclaimed, half standing, wanting to get his mind on other things than June's physical attractiveness. It was literally seducing his body.

"Can I finish my drink?" she asked, eyeing him in a strange, flirting way. Her eyes swept up and down his body, taking in every inch of it; and there was an outward desire in them that she couldn't hide.

"Okay. But make it fast!" he demanded curtly.

"You don't have to be angry," she pouted, unhurt sounding.

"Not your fault. Well, yes... it is...never mind!"

106

"I rather think the drinks are getting to us, don't you?" she offered, brightly.

"What're you talking about?"

"Under other circumstances, a man and woman, like the two of us, sitting in a cocktail lounge, sipping martinis, might very well find themselves –"

"Don't go there."

"Why not? We're human. And, like I said, Bob, I really do find you quite a nice guy. The kind I'd love to date, under the right circumstances."

"That's rather...blunt," Robert mused, suddenly finding his eyes literally racing over her body, caressing her, mentally wondering what it must be like to feel her flesh flush against his own.

"I can be honest, when honesty is required." She reached out and touched his hand. The contact was startlingly exciting. "Admit it, Bob, we both feel the same thing...some people are just kinda naturally attracted to one another. And...besides, we don't want to rush off half-cocked...now do we? Sometimes a little careful thinking..."

She touched his arm. "I really don't want anything horrid to happen to you."

"It won't!"

"You can't be sure."

"Well maybe you should just—"

"Don't say it. I'm staying with you. Maybe your...*safety switch*. Two can be better than one, anyway."

He sighed, frustrated. Somehow it seemed that she was more than merely flirting or being seductive. It was as if the woman was attempting to distract him. The idea that she'd get into bed with him to stop any dangerous act on his part was somewhat startling.

He pushed that thought out of his mind. Imagination.

"Let's get out of here!"

It only took her a few moments to finish the drink and then she stood and moved from the booth.

As they walked from the saloon, Robert was aware of the nearness of June; he couldn't get the feeling of her closeness out of his mind, or the knowledge that she was purposely making it a point to walk near him. Once, accidentally, her hip brushed his and he experienced an electric physical reaction. He could feel tingling needles stab through every cell in his body. His eyes shot momentarily in her direction. There was a pleased expression on her face, and he knew that she had felt it too.

And she had all but read his thoughts.

They moved out into the lobby of the hotel and then toward the elevator. He would give it one more try this evening and then drop June off at her apartment, where she belonged.

In the elevator June stood close to him and then suddenly, without warning, leaned closer and placed a kiss on his lips. For a moment neither of them did anything. The touch of her lips had been too overwhelming. Then just as abruptly she stepped away, a red flush moving up her face.

"I'm sorry, Bob!" was all that she said. But the words were choked in her voice.

Somehow he didn't feel she was really sorry.

They didn't say anything for a long while, not until they were opposite the doorway to Turner's apartment.

Robert rang the bell and then waited. Silence.

He rang again and then sighed when there wasn't any answer.

"Okay—let's forget it for tonight!" he decided, turning toward June and looking her full in the eyes. He didn't move; all at once he found himself unable to move. June was staring at him with a warm, tender expression on her face; but also the expression of a woman suddenly swept up in a wave of passion and desire. There was a fiery look in her eyes as they stared up into his.

"Let's go!" he demanded, reaching out and turning her around. That was a mistake. The soft giving of her supple shoulder sparked through him like an electric shock. He'd never experienced such a reaction before. Maybe it was the liquor? Maybe something else deep down inside him that was trying to get out? He didn't know. And suddenly he decided not to care or question. There were things that couldn't be reasoned out; there were things that defied reason and logic or moral rights and wrongs. He knew that he wanted June. And he knew that she felt the same way. And maybe it didn't matter as anything but a momentary flirtation and seduction, a much needed orgiastic desire. They said that sex and death could many time be related in a perversely strange way. One last time before dying; one last moment of ecstasy.

"Let's go to my place," was all that he said.

She just nodded, and followed him down the hall toward the elevator.

There wasn't anything to say; there wasn't anything that either of them could do about what was happening. It was out of their hands. The desire, heated passion, physical need was too strong, too powerful to be reasoned out or battled with. It needed consumption.

Tomorrow he would worry about the reasons. Tomorrow he would find some rationalization to justify what he was about to do.

All he could think of, all the way to his place, was: *forgive me Carol, please forgive me.*

* * * * * * *

They stopped off at a liquor store to get a bottle of whisky. Neither of them had said anything from the moment he had made his suggestion; neither of them said anything until they were in his room with the door closed and locked behind them.

"What do you want?" he asked grimly, indicating the bottle of whiskey.

"Not much choice!" June laughed, coming closer to him and sliding her arms around his neck. "Come on, don't be so silly about this. There's nothing wrong with it. When two adults want one another—sometimes it just has to happen. No questions asked; no strings."

"Let's not talk about it!" he snapped, gently pushing her away and moving to the bathroom and getting the two glasses. He half filled them with liquor then topped that with water and returned to her. He handed one to June and then took several swallows from his own glass.

"No ice. Okay?"

"Who wants ice? I don't want to be cooled off, Bob...not that way."

He was already sorry that he had made his suggestion, but there wasn't anything that he could do about it, then or now. Maybe it was just a frustrated need for a woman's body! He didn't care to reason it out; and he didn't care to think about it. Booze it up and then knock it up with the broad. It would be as simple as that!

The liquor settled in his stomach and then started slowly to race out its numbing fingers through his body. It reached up to his brain and soothed the torment there. Gently soothing the ache and guilt of what he was doing.

"You're certainly grim!" June observed, moving closer to Robert. She smiled, reaching out a delicate hand and caressing his cheek. The action and contact returned the fire and desire. It was electric—the shock that jarred through every cell in him, firing through his body.

He didn't think about what he was doing—he just did it.

Reaching out, he violently yanked June against him, her drink spilling over his clothing; but neither of them noticed. Their lips met in one explosive contact, parted, trembling and moist. The touch of her tongue against his ripped all thoughts from his mind except one: satisfaction of his body's need.

For a long time they stood there in the middle of the room, exploring each other's mouths, locked tightly together. He tried to blind himself of everything other than the sensation of her lovely body, so soft, full, warm. He could feel the supple give of her breasts as they pressed anxiously against him; he could feel her hips surge hard and eagerly. How long the kiss lasted he didn't know; he lost all awareness of time. The only sensation that he felt was the delightful sweet excitement of her tongue as it worked rhythmically with his.

The heat built, flooding through their bodies, moving them tighter and tighter together, until they were squirming and desperately seeking harder union. His breathing was short and heavy when they pulled away, looking at each other.

"Well!" she finally exclaimed, "You sure are something!"

He just nodded toward the bed. She caught the meaning and didn't hesitate. June turned her back to him and said: "Unzip my dress?"

He reached out and slowly moved the zipper down to the point where it ended at the top of her buttocks. Then he suddenly slipped his hands under the cloth and, reaching around her body, filled his fingers with her full breast, his lips digging into the whiteness of her throat.

A sigh of pleasure purred from her lips and she leaned back against him, pressing eagerly.

And a sob of anguish pain rushed through him, shattering all thought. He simply wanted to escape into her arms, flesh, and smother himself into her as fully as possible. Escape reality for just a moment.

They stood there for awhile, his fingers caressing and fondling as her body squirmed in response against his. Then he slid his hands back around to the clasp of her bra. A moment later the dress and bra were on the floor and she was leaning back against him again, his fingers caressing and working on her breasts, first tenderly, and then savagely. Suddenly she twisted in his arms and they crushed together, brutally biting at each other's lips, their tongues rapidly moving. For a long time they surged and squirmed against each other, then June started

112

pulling his jacket off, and then his shirt, and a moment later they both stood before each other, completely nude.

"You're beautiful," he gasped, looking at her, the breath caught in him. She was even more beautiful than Carol. Thoughts of his wife choked in his mind for only a second, as June eagerly pulled him toward the bed. A moment later the two of them were full length on the bed, tightly holding each other.

A sob of pain ebbed up through him and his eyes flooded with tears. Gentle, tender hands covered his cheeks, lips kissed him.

"Its okay, Bob," she murmured, understandingly. She pulled him to her breasts. "Here...just enjoy me."

She held him tenderly at first, then he became aware of her full warm breasts against his lips. For a very long time he didn't move. He never knew when they started making love.

He was suddenly simply holding her softly in his arms, literally comforted by the very warmth of her flesh.

For a long time they didn't do anything but just lie there, breathing heavily, taking in the excitement of being so close, so intimate. Then slowly, very slowly, the desire built into wild animal need, shattering all resistance. Nothing could hold back the demanding flood that rushed over him. After than it was just an endless series of sensations that drowned his very soul.

CHAPTER THIRTEEN

When Robert Bradley awoke the next morning it was with the sense of depression. For a long while he lay back in bed, thinking, not opening his eyes, in a half state of sleep. Memory of June's raging body against his was still vivid in his mind. He couldn't get her fiery lovemaking out of his head. Her lips that had quivered delightfully against his; her breasts, giving and responsive to his every kiss. She had a wildness that overwhelmed him beyond all control!

But there was the other thought. The tormented pain of knowing that he had taken another woman to bed and made love to her so soon after his wife's death. That pain raged through his mind, whipping the guilt until he almost wanted to cry from it. The whole thing had been a sin against Carol. It had made his feelings for her cheap and coarse! How could a man, possessed with such a strong desire for revenge be able to take another woman into his arms?

He opened his eyes.

The bed next to him was empty. Anxiously he sat up, looking around. Mixed emotions flooded through him.

"June!" he called out.

114

"Oh, are you awake?" June's voice called from the bathroom. "I'll be right out." A moment later she stepped into the room, only a towel draped around her waist. Her breasts, large and beautiful, stood out full and self-supporting. "I was wondering when you would awaken."

A groan sounded from his lips as he stood and moved past June, going into the bathroom and closing the door behind him.

Looking into the mirror he tried to figure out what kind of man he was. *What right did he have to make love to another woman? What kind of woman was June, anyway?*

Suddenly he realized that he really didn't really know anything about June. If he looked at the whole thing realistically, he could class her as a cheap little tramp that gave out her body to any man that came along. Or maybe a free spirit? He hardly knew her, yet she had openly offered herself. All he had had to do was suggest that they go to his place, and she had been more than willing!

But then, he thought, look at the kind of people that she ran around with!

Ruth Kirby!

Robert was pretty sure that she was connected with gangsters. He was very sure that Jake Turner was in the rackets—and that the man had something to do with Carol's death.

What'd that make his dead wife?

Bitterness choked in his throat as he started washing his face. Bitterness of what had happened the night before. Bitterness at what he was thinking of right then. For suddenly he realized that his thoughts concerning June could just as easily be tar-

115

geting his dead wife. Carol who had gone to Holly-wood to become a big star and had only managed to star in the bedrooms of a lot of men! Ending up in hotels with any bastard with a bill!

Robert's guts hurt suddenly. He wanted to vomit them out into the sink. For a long moment his hands clawed at the sink, his stomach all but retching, but finally he gained control of the anguished nerves and muscles of his body.

After a few minutes he stepped out of the bath-room and started getting dressed. He ignored the presence of the woman as much as he could. But he found himself glancing every once in a while in June's direction, caressing the supple curves of her breasts with his eyes. She had a body that demanded to be taken and a look in her eyes that gave open in-vitation! At least to him, at this moment.

It was half an hour before June was dressed, and seeing her nude breasts didn't help Robert's physi-cal reactions to her. He wanted to forget, but sight of her made it impossible.

Finally the two of them walked from the room. Neither had said anything since June's first greeting when he had awakened. It wasn't until they were in his car, driving along the Hollywood freeway, to-ward June's place, that she interrupted the long si-lence.

"What's wrong?"

It took a few moments for Robert to answer that question, and then it was bitterly. "What do you think?"

"I only hope that it doesn't have anything to do with me. I thought you were great!"

"So I was great!" Robert snapped, angrily.

116

"Don't you understand? Carol just died. That shouldn't have happened."

June remained silent all the way back to her apartment.

"You don't have to take me up," she said.

He was glad to be rid of her, so he just nodded and then gunned the car away. He didn't know exactly what he planned to do. First he needed some food, a little coffee, and then he could follow up the Jake Turner lead. *But where to find the man?* It was like trying to find the old needle in one hell of a gigantic hay stack, and he just wasn't a professional private eye! He didn't know where to start.

Ruth Kirby. He knew where she worked. That might be a good idea. He could go to her and get the information that was necessary. After breakfast and a cup of coffee.

* * * * * * *

Ruth felt a sense of frustration as she sat behind her desk. The evening with Jake had been an emotionally unsettling one. The fact that she had no course but to go along with him left her with a feeling that she was not only selling Robert Bradley down the drain, but also Carol and herself. Mainly herself. There were such things as moral rights and wrongs, and she now realized that in the last years she'd forgotten about them for the sake of money! Now for the first time she was beginning to wonder if it had been worth it. But it was too late to back down now; there wasn't any pulling out. Turning on Jake would mean instant death! She didn't fool herself about that; even if the man had accepted her word, he didn't trust her any more, and she was walking on a thin line that could suddenly disappear if she wasn't careful!

The plans were simple enough. Set Robert Bradley up for a trap that would leave him all but dead. And there just wasn't anything that she could do about it.

The hours before noon were long and tiring. The thoughts raced through her mind, filled her with a sense of self shame and disgust. She had let herself be sucked into a terrible trap, from which there was no escape but death—and she didn't want to die. If nothing else, she didn't want to die!

She was just getting ready to leave for lunch when Robert Bradley stepped into her office.

"Hello, Ruth, I have a few things I want to ask you about," he told her in a stiff, forced voice. "And I'm going to want answers this time! Ones that will count."

For a moment she frowned at him, then slowly she stood. "Not here. We'll go out to lunch. I'll talk to you then."

The two of them left the office, not speaking. She led him down to the street floor and then into the building's dining room. There was a cocktail lounge and they walked into it, taking a dark booth in the far corner.

"I'm going to need a few drinks—first!" she stated, forcefully.

"Anything you want. But let's not play any games, this time. I'm a little tired of the run-around you've been giving me." The expression in his eyes was hard and determined.

They sat for a long time, not talking, waiting for

118

their drinks. He had a martini and she had ordered a scotch on the rocks. After the drinks had arrived and she had downed half of hers, Ruth felt a little better. She knew what had to be done, and even if she didn't like it, *she would have to do it.*

For a long while she looked at Robert, feeling a sense of sorrow for the man. He just didn't know what he was doing; he was up against powers that he couldn't ever combat, alone. And he was alone.

"What do you want?" she asked, trying to make her voice sound as if she were reluctant to say anything, as if she were going to play it careful.

"I want to know how to get hold of Jake Turner!" Robert stated matter-of-factly, leaning across the table and staring into her eyes.

"What are you talking about?'

"Cut the crap!" he snapped. "I'm not such a square as you might think! I've put two and two together and come up with the magic answer of four."

"Why do you want to see Jake?"

"I think you know why. And I think you are going to tell me where to get hold of him!"

"Look, Robert, can't you forget all this? Please! You don't know what you're up against. These boys are going to—"

"Cut it!" he ordered his face tightened into a hard cold knot. His eyes narrowed. "I know where his apartment is—but I want to know where he can be located. I want his office address, his phone, anywhere I can get hold of him. I want to see him today—and that's the end of it!"

She sat for a while, looking blankly at him. This was better than Jake had hoped for. She was able to send this poor slob right into the trap without any trouble! It was almost too easy. But suddenly Ruth realized that there wasn't anything that she could ever have done. Robert Bradley was a stubborn man and would finish what he started. She had just been wasting her time trying to pull him off the track. Anyway, she'd done everything humanly possible.

"Okay, buster-boy, I see you just want to get yourself killed! That's what will happen, you know. But I'll arrange a meeting. You come to my apartment tonight—Jake will be there!"

CHAPTER FOURTEEN

After he left Ruth Kirby, Robert had found a place on Main Street where he could get a gun. The next thing had been simply bribing the owner to sell him the gun without a permit. It was an under-the-counter arrangement. The gun was a snub-nosed .38 that he was easily able to hide in his pocket. It showed slightly, but nobody who didn't have a trained eye could tell that it was a gun.

The next thing was to kill time. He went to his apartment and slept, setting the clock for seven-thirty. When it rang he sat up, dressed, washed his face and walked down to where he had parked his car.

Thirty minutes later he was stepping toward the door to Ruth Kirby's apartment. There was a feeling of excitement rushing through his body. He felt sure that this was the moment that he had come to Hollywood for. But he planned to make sure before he killed Jake Turner. He planned to be sure that this was the man responsible for Carol's death!

He only hesitated at the front of the door long enough to place his hand in the pocket where the gun was. Then he rang the bell.

The door opened immediately. A tall, lean-faced young man looked out, a deadly grin on his face.

"Who're you?" the man demanded.

"None of your damned business. Are Ruth and Turner here?"

"Turner is. You're our man!' The door opened the rest of the way. Robert stepped in and it was closed behind him.

All the lights were on. There were three men in the room beside the barrel-chested man that he recognized as Jake Turner.

Turner looked up as Robert stepped in, a smile on his face. He extended his hand, walking over and greeting Robert. "Well if it isn't Mr. Gordon—oh, that was just a little game that Ruth and you and June played on me. That's right, you are Robert Bradley, husband of Carol Benton—isn't that right?"

Robert ignored the hand, looking straight into Turner's eyes. "What're all the others here for?"

Turner didn't answer the question, instead only nodded.

Before Robert could do anything he was grabbed from behind by the man who had answered the door. A moment later another stepped up and searched his pockets, coming up with the .38, which he extended to Turner.

Jake smiled, taking hold of the gun and pointing it toward Robert. "My, my, but isn't this out of place for a country hick!" He laughed and then nodded again. Robert was released. "What in the world were you doing with a thing like this? A man like you with a temper could be very dangerous with a gun. I take it that you have a permit for it?"

"That's none of your business!' Robert snapped, standing stiffly.

122

"Now, I wouldn't say that. I would think it was very much my business, being a loyal, law-abiding citizen." He chuckled and dramatically cocked the weapon that was still pointed in Robert's direction. "But I guess you have a lot to learn. Yes, I think that you have one hell of a lot to learn."

The man's attitude changed suddenly, becoming deadly serious. "I heard that you wanted to see me. But I don't think that you knew that we wanted to see you! There are a few things that country boys like you have to learn about the big city. And I'm here to see that you learn them well." He paused for a moment, and then smiled. "But first, how'd you like a drink? There's no reason for us to be all business-like, now is there?"

"I don't want a drink!"

"I think you'll be needing one before the evening is finished."

"I don't know what your game is, but you aren't scaring me!" Robert said stiffly.

"Oh, did you hear that, boys? This guy doesn't scare easily. Maybe we should prove our point!" He snapped his fingers.

For an instant Robert had a flashing idea of what was about to happen. His muscles reacted fast. But not fast enough. Before he could do anything he was grabbed again from behind. He struggled, but the man was stronger and had the advantage. Then suddenly the training that he'd learned in the service helped him, going into automatic action.

He twisted and whipped around, knocking the man off balance. A second later he whipped around to face the other two. But he was an instant too late. A fist made contact with his jaw and another

123

smashed into the pit of his stomach. He doubled over, and a moment later he was being held by two pairs of arms. A man was on each side of him. The third was facing him.

"You damned cowards!" he cried. A slashing blow whipped his face to one side. Another fist hit the other cheek and a third hammered into his gut again.

"That's enough, boys—for right now!" Jake's voice sounded out of the haze.

Robert was released; he half slumped to the floor, dazed and spitting blood.

"Now are you a little scared, Mr. Bradley?" Turner's smooth voice asked pleasantly. "Now would you like that drink?"

"What kind of goddam bastards are you?" Robert blurted out, finally gaining control of his muscles and standing erect again. For the first time he realized exactly what he was up against! He was afraid, but he was mad—madder than he'd ever been before!

"I think I can imagine what you are thinking. But that's the first lesson I wanted to teach you, my friend. We don't play fair. This isn't any game. This is a life and death matter—and we play for keeps. We don't care how we win or what has to be done in order to win. If it takes three men to soften somebody up who is getting in our way, then that is what is done. The morals and ethics that you read in books—that is just a lot of crap! You won't find it in real life! You got me?"

Robert stood for a long while, looking at the men. He was helpless against such numbers. Right now he would have to play it by ear and see where it

124

got him. The cards were stacked on the other side. He would have to wait and bide his time.

"Okay, what's your game?"

Turner laughed and then said: "I thought that you arranged this meeting. What I want to know is what *your* game is. And then we'll see what my game is." He paused and then said in an almost friendly voice. "How about that drink?"

Robert shook his head angrily, waving his hand in the air. "You go to hell with your drinks!"

A hard expression showed on Turner's face, then he slowly smiled. "Have it your way!" Turner nodded to the man nearest the small home bar. "Fix me a shot of scotch." He looked back at Robert then. "Well, I think the next move is yours."

Suddenly Robert didn't know what to say. He'd come here to get information from Turner. Beat it out of the man if possible. The tables were turned and there just wasn't a direct way to get to the point of his questioning now.

"Maybe I can help you a little, in case that slapping around froze your tongue," Turner nastily. "Isn't it something to do with your Carol Benton?"

"You bastard!"

"Watch your talk, sonny-boy!" the man snapped, frowning. Then his voice became silky smooth once more as he continued. "It seems, from what Ruth has told me, and from my information sources, that you are here in town to find the person responsible for your wife's sudden death. Am I right?" He didn't wait for an answer, but continued. "Now, it would seem that the trail has led you this far, and, strangely enough, you don't seem to be very talkative. But maybe that's because we took your 'teeth' out!" Turner indicated the .38 in his hands. "It's a shame that a man has to have such a thing to give him courage. I thought that you were much different from that. A different man. But, it just goes to show..."

"Okay, Mr. Turner, so you're in control. I came here to find out something and I plan on finding it out! You seem to have some connection with it, so maybe you can tell me a little bit about it."

Turner had the scotch now and he sipped it carefully. For a while he didn't say anything, but just looked through Robert. Then suddenly he seemed to make up his mind. "Okay, I'll tell you what. I'm going to level with you. But I'll warn you, it won't do you any good. It will only make this a little more interesting. You'll know everything that you came here to find out and won't be able to do a damn thing about it!" He stopped to sip the scotch and then continued: "First, your wife was a nice young thing when she came to Hollywood. Then she got into the wrong crowd. These silly little girls who come to town thinking they're so full of talent that the world is just shivering and shaking to sign them up. Stupid. It takes more than talent, good looks, and connections. Timing. And so much more that they don't even begin to understand. It is a fool's game.

"After many frustrating months of getting nowhere fast, she started playing along. We had all the right connections for women like her. Finally she ended up giving out. Another stupid move. Little men with impressive titles over their offices have couches made just for having young women suck up to them. No different from any other business; only

126

that here the stakes are high; very high. The competition very, very hard to go up against. Girls like her are tossed from office to office with dumb implied promises made. Give me some fun on the couch and you'll get a small walk on, maybe....

"Then after the right contact was made she was convinced that she could do much better selling her body. We wait until the girl hits rock bottom and then present her with the right deal. She worked for the Syndicate, getting big money for pleasing out-of-town businessmen. Half of it went to the Syndicate. She was kept in fine jewels and furs—coming out of her earned money. Lived in high class surroundings. Being a beautiful woman she finally attracted certain important people, and being intelligent she played things right and ended up putting out to one of the really big boys—and he took a fancy to her. From then on she stayed with him. All of a sudden she disappeared. This man didn't like being walked out on. But there were other things that came up. Also she had a lot of information that we didn't want to have given to the government. Then two things happened. One, a new deal, which she knew about slightly, was going through—and then the government was putting a Senate probe into our affairs.

"Carol Benton was on the top of a list of possible witnesses. There was only one thing to do. Get to her before the government got to her. I was given orders and they were followed out."

Robert stood there, silently listening, stunned and shocked by what he heard. The cold bloodedness of it all; the cool, matter-of-fact way that Turner made his announcements. Then suddenly

127

something broke through his shell of resistance. The civilized side of him exploded into nothing, leaving only the raw animal insanity, naked and exposed and expressing itself.

Robert wasn't aware at first of what he was doing.

One moment he was standing, listening, and the next he was racing at Turner. Before anybody could do anything his fingers were around the man's throat, squeezing violently. Squeezing with all the fury and hate and disgust that had been building in him ever since his wife's death.

He didn't think of what could happen to him; he didn't think that he couldn't possibly have time to kill the man before the others could get him under control. All he thought was *kill*.

KILL!

He didn't even care if he lived or died, just so he took this bastard with him. It was a hopeless wish; a desperate play. But obviously Jake expected to kill him, in any case, after having offered up that story.

He was aware of Turner's eyes popping and his face turning red in pain and the sound of the choking gasp in the man's throat as he tried to get air into his lungs.

Then something came down on Robert's head. At first he didn't react; he continued to squeeze. Then another hammer-like object descended onto the back of his head, and blackness exploded before his vision, and he slumped to the floor.

CHAPTER FIFTEEN

June Edmondson looked across the cocktail table at Ruth. The other woman's face was deeply lined with worry, her lips drooping as she sipped the fourth martini.

"What's bothering you, Ruthie?" she asked, taking another light swallow of her second high-ball.

"Nothing! Nothing that could concern you!" Ruth snapped angrily, biting her lower lip nervously.

"There's *something...*"

"Just lay off"

"Look, if it's anything that I can help you with..."

Ruth laughed, her head bending back, her eyes widening, almost insanely. "You *kidding,* you innocent little thing? If you only knew!"

"Knew *what?*"

"Oh, shut up, you little slut!" Ruth exploded, finishing her cocktail and looking around for the waiter.

"Look, I don't have to take that kind of talk from anybody!" June exclaimed, standing, anger flooding up through her.

Ruth's expression changed. A startled look came into her eyes. "I'm sorry, June. It's just that I have things on my mind."

June softened inside suddenly. She felt sorry for Ruth, and didn't know why. The woman was bothered about something, but she couldn't imagine what. When Ruth had come home that evening she'd suggested they go out for dinner and then cocktails, saying that she was nervous and had to get out. From what little June knew of the woman, it was unlike Ruth. But she had gone along with the idea. She had things she was worried about, too. She was scared to death about Robert Bradley. And then there was that other thing: she knew that there was *more* than just sexual desire that she felt for him. Maybe she was falling in love with the man.

She directed her attention to Ruth. The woman had ordered another round of drinks and was already beginning to work on her martini.

"You know, June," Ruth said quietly, "This is one hell of a nasty life!"

June remained silent.

"Now you take that little fool, Robert Bradley. He's going to get himself all but killed—" Ruth broke off, her eyes widening.

"What are you talking about?" June demanded.

"Nothing—just that he's nosing into things that he doesn't have any right to…"

"Isn't there any way?" June asked in a pleading voice. "Any way to stop him?"

"Ah, that's being taken care of!" Ruth's eyes were glassy, and the way she talked was in much too loud a voice.

'What do you mean?"

"He'll be stopped—that's for sure! Jake and the boys are making sure of that!"

130

"He's not—" June cried in alarm.

"Oh, they won't kill him. Just push him around—beat him up a bit—make him wish they *did* kill him."

"Can't...can't you stop them? Can't you tell them to leave him alone?" June pleaded, anxiously, feeling a frantic sickness in her gut.

"Oh, but that's too late, my dear."

June felt her face go white with terror. *"What do you mean?"*

"What's it to you, anyway. For God's sake, June, he's just a stupid fool, nosing into things he shouldn't be bothering with."

"His wife—"

"Oh, for God's sake. So she's dead and her child is dead and a million other people are dead. People die every day. The only smart thing in life is to keep alive—survive anyway you can. Cause if you don't look out for yourself, you're the one that ends up six feet under sooner than you can blink an eye!"

"What's happening?" June cried. "Tell me! Damn it!"

"You sound like you actually care about the ass!"

"I do!" She cried. "And I don't want anything happening to him."

"Well, you're too late for that, now!"

"What're you saying?"

"They're taking care of that right now—in our apartment!"

Ruth suddenly sobered, stunned by what she had said, realizing that she'd said too much. She stood, reaching out an arm toward June. "Oh, God. Forget what I told you!"

June was already on her feet.

"We have to call the police! We have to stop it!" she half screamed.

"You don't know what you're talking about! If we called the police—and Jake found out that it was my fault—he'd kill me!"

June didn't care. She didn't care about anything; or even what they might do to her! She suddenly realized only one thing: she had to help Robert in any way she could. She couldn't let Robert take a set-up beating and not do anything about. Suddenly everything inside her cried for one thing: *Call the police.*

Before Ruth could do anything to stop her, June was rushing across the saloon toward the telephone. There had been another revelation that had snapped into her awareness. She didn't want anything to do with Hollywood—with the life that she had almost allowed herself to get sucked into; the trap from which there would be no escape if she let it close in on her!

She would do the only thing that she could do. Call the police!

* * * * * *

Robert Bradley felt the world slowly spin back into being. The blackness ebbed away painfully. At first he couldn't remember where he was, or what had happened. Then suddenly it all returned to him like a slap across the face.

He jerked, trying to get up.

His eyes opened and he looked around him.

He was lying on the floor. Jake Turner was sitting in a chair just a few feet away, holding the .38 in his hand, the barrel pointed in Robert's direction.

"I see that you finally came out of it," the man said in a deadly tight voice.

Robert spotted the other three men a few feet away from him, ready to leap forward.

"You know, my boy, you have just made the biggest mistake of your short life. I was only going to push you around a little—try to scare you off. *But now I'm going to simply kill you.*"

Robert felt a sickness throb through him; a complete sense of defeat. *What had it all gotten him?* In a trap without any escape hatch! He didn't mind dying if he took Turner with him; he didn't mind that at all. He had lost all his will to live when Carol died. But to die, knowing what he now knew, and not being able to do anything about it—that was a dirty trick of fate! He had found out what he had come to Hollywood to discover. What Carol had been doing those ten years, who had killed her, and why. Then there was the other point. Turner was only the trigger man—or had hired the trigger men. To get complete revenge he would have to kill the trigger men and Turner and the dirty bastard slob that had given the order. Where would it have all ended?

But that didn't count now!

He looked at Turner and felt the bitter taste of defeat.

'So kill me!" he snapped slowly standing

He had hardly gotten to his feet when two of the men grabbed him from behind. He didn't even try to struggle. There just wasn't any point to it anymore.

Only a fool didn't know when he was beaten.

"Oh, it won't be as simple as all that. First of all we have a few things to take care of, my friend. We won't make this just a matter of killing you. It's going to be a slow, painful thing."

"Aren't you afraid that the neighbors might hear?"

"They haven't heard anything so far. I picked this place as a meeting spot because the walls are soundproof. This is an expensive apartment. Ruth has a lot of money and we see to it that she keeps having a lot of money. Her so-called job is a cover-up for things she does for us. So I don't think that there will be any problems. The only thing is that I'm sorry that I won't be around to see it happen. I find it a good idea to never be around when somebody gets killed—it might not be good for business."

He stood and started for the door, then paused.

"Just one more thing," Jake stated, turning to look at Robert again, "if you hadn't been such a fool as to touch me—well, I think you might have lived through the beating. But now the boys are going to have a field day." He directed his next statement to the three men. "I want him dumped in the deepest part of the ocean, so that he doesn't turn up for one hell of a long time! Like never!" With that parting remark he opened the door and left.

"I think we better give Jake a little chance to get out of the place. About half an hour!" the third man stated, stepping forward and smashing his gun across the side of Robert's head.

Blackness exploded.

He ebbed out of it slowly; then as awareness

came he felt a sickness in his gut. He had to do something; he just couldn't let them kill him without a struggle!

So far he hadn't moved, that much he was sure of.

They wouldn't realize that he was conscious yet.

All of a sudden he sprang to his feet. His eyes were wide open and he took in his surroundings in one sweep. The three were only feet away and they had quickly reacted to his abrupt move.

Robert swung at the first man. But missed. The injury from the beating that his body and head had already taken had set in, weakening his swing and reaction, causing a sudden dizziness to cloud around him. Once it had cleared in his brain, he was being held by two of the men, and the third was standing in front of him, grinning.

"Well, well, now, our boy still has some fight left in him! But that won't last long!"

A hand slapped across Robert's face. It was only a stinging blow. It slapped again, this time harder, whipping his head to one side. Then a fist slammed into the pit of his stomach. He tried to double over, but the strong hands holding him kept his body erect, as a steel hammer smashed into his nose. He felt crunching and the moistness of blood. His face was numb.

But it had only started.

He lost track of the hits. Yet he was conscious of one thing. First they would come hard, and then turn into slaps, giving him time to recover, then they would smash brutally into his stomach.

He felt his guts erupt from his throat out past his mouth, as a knee jerked into his groin. Blackness formed before his eyes and then cleared as a jarring fist smashed his lips into his teeth, cutting them. He felt the blood gush into his mouth and tried to spit it out, but another fist shot against his lips again, forcing the salty redness to float down his chin.

Another knee rammed into his groin and he felt all consciousness slip away. How long he was out he didn't know. But the next thing he was aware of was voices. Then the soft touch of a woman's hand on his forehead. He groaned and tried to open his eyes. They barely made it. Then closed. But in that one second he saw the face and form of June Edmondson leaning very close to him. He thought he had seen tears in her eyes, tears of pain and sorrow, but he wasn't sure. He didn't know what had happened and hadn't the energy or will to even care.

A voice sounded softly to his left; it was deep and male and kindly. "It's a wonder that he's alive. Here, give me his arm—this will take care of him for a while, until we get him to the hospital."

A needle pricked him and then blackness slowly and caressingly ebbed around Robert, cutting out all awareness; all thought and all pain.

* * * * * * *

Ruth had sat, terrified, as June walked across the saloon, toward the phone booth. But there wasn't anything that she could do. And deep down inside she had the feeling that June was doing the right thing; she didn't want to have a man's life on her hands! But it also meant that now her life was in danger! Once Jake found out what had happened— he would blame her.

136

Ruth's head was still spinning from the drinks when she finally decided that the best thing she could do was to suddenly and completely disappear. It was her only chance to escape with her life. Her whole career was finished, that much she now knew.

At least for a good long time; or if she could find a way to explain things to Jake Turner. Or if everything worked out all right—but she doubted that would happen.

Disappear and watch the events and see what happened; that was all that she could do.

Exit Ruth Kirby!

CHAPTER SIXTEEN

Robert wasn't aware of anything for a long while. He was floating in time and space where nothingness existed—neither time nor space. Then slowly he became aware of *being*. Then finally thought and shape came into focus. He didn't know where he was, or remember anything about himself. He was only aware of *thinking* and *being*.

Then a desire moved through him. A desire for *somebody*. At first he couldn't tell who it was. Then finally, very slowly, a face came into view before his eyes, giving light to the darkness.

It was the face of *Carol*. But he couldn't place the name. Not at first. All he knew was when he saw the face he felt emotion. Love and need. Desire so strong that he wanted to shout out.

The face smiled at him. "Hello, darling," it said.

"Hello, Carol," he said back. It was then that he remembered who she was. "Where have you been?"

"Does that matter? The only thing that matters is that I'm here, with you. Take me in your arms. Let me feel the life pulse of you. Let me feel your kisses on my naked flesh. Let me feel the thrill of your lips on my breasts, warm and moist, caressing, kissing. Let me feel your body on mine, heated with passion, shaking with desire, burning with love!"

138

Suddenly Carol was standing before him, naked and beautiful, desirable and warm with life and the joy of life. She moved into his arms, her whole body caressing his.

They held each other for a long while, just feeling the nearness of each other, like they had done so many times in the past. Then he caressed her white throat with his lips.

"Love me with your lips. Love me with your body. Love me with your soul!" she said in a husky voice, pushing harder against him. Moving her hips hard and violently against his.

For a moment they explored each other's mouth, then she pulled away.

He looked at her, startled and shocked.

Her face was changing, her blonde hair changing color. Turning red. Her forehead widening slightly. Then all at once he was looking into the face of June Edmondson.

"What are you doing here?" he screamed in terror. "Where's Carol?"

"She's dead. I'm alive. She's gone. I'm here for you to take. To do with as you please. Cover my body with kisses. Take my body and feel it warm to your touch. *Feel the life and fire in me!*"

She pulled herself against him, sighing. And he reacted savagely. He crushed her hard against his body. He felt the warmth of her. He covered her lips with kisses. Her breasts. Her body. Then he stopped.

The guilt. She wasn't Carol. She wasn't the one who counted! He couldn't make love to her. He couldn't caress her body. He had no right to kiss her. He had no right to take her in his arms.

Carol. Only Carol.

But Carol was dead. He couldn't have her again. And he did have to live. What was wrong with making love to June?

June was a woman who gave herself to men. Just like Carol had. Just like his dear dead wife had.

The emotions welled up through him, a confusion of love and hate, fury and disgust, anguish mixing with all the tenderness and passion a person could possibly feel.

He wanted to survive. He wanted to live. He wanted to forgive Carol. Life was too complex to be nothing more than black and white. Survival was all that counted in the end. Somehow survive.

He reached for her.

But she was gone.

There was only blackness around him. A blackness that was starting to throb. Throb with light; red light.

With the throbbing light came pain. With each throb came a terrible vise that squeezed his body and then released it. And then squeezed once more and then again and then again. Over and over, each time more painful. Each time the light becoming stronger and the blackness becoming gray.

Finally the pain was continuous. A pain that kept aching all over his body; a pain that didn't stop.

He wanted to *scream* in the agony of it, but he couldn't.

Suddenly he was aware of voices. They were far away and at first he couldn't make out what they were saying. Then slowly they gained volume.

"...He's coming out of it now..."

"Oh, God—I've been so—"

"He'll be okay after a long, long rest. He's lucky to be alive as it is!"

He opened his eyes. The action hurt, but once they were open he was able to keep them open. He was looking up at the ceiling. For a long time, he couldn't understand where he was, or what had happened last. Then slowly memory came painfully back.

But why wasn't he dead? What had saved him? His mind screamed the question; but nobody answered it.

"Bob," a woman's voice said gently at his side. "Bob."

He tried to turn, but couldn't. He moved his eyes in the direction of the voice.

June Edmondson was leaning over him, her red hair flowing over her shoulders, a sad, concerned look in her eyes.

"What...what are...you doing?"

"Don't try to talk. I just want you to know that I'm here. I'll be here always, as long as you'll let me be. Don't talk now."

He couldn't understand what she was saying; what she meant by her words; why she was saying it.

But his mind was too tired to think; his mind was too tired to reason or try to reason. He sighed and tried to relax. Relax and worry about things later.

The thought drifted out to nothingness as slowly all consciousness faded.

* * * * * * *

Jake Turner sat in his office, in his apartment. Red fury clouded his features. "There's only one way that the police could have been called in on this—*Ruth.* Ruth Kirby!" he snapped, looking at the man opposite him.

"What you going to do about it, boss?" the man asked, grim-faced.

"There are several things that have to be done about it.

"First, see to it that we get a smart lawyer. None of the ones connected to the Syndicate. I want this to be a clean case. The two men that were arrested...I want them out on bail in twenty-four hours!"

"Yes, boss."

"And another thing..." Turner paused for a moment, in thought. "This is going to look bad to the boys in the Syndicate. Ruth has made a very bad mistake and we can't take the fall for it."

For a long time Turner didn't say anything. His face was tense in concentration. There was a deep sadness around his eyes. Then he made up his mind. "Find Ruth. I don't know where she's disappeared to—but find her *and kill her*."

"What about this Bradley guy?"

"Leave him alone for the time being. We can't follow it up right now. It is too dangerous. Just leave him alone!" Turner sat back, a deep tired sigh breaking from his lips. "We'll deal with him...no matter how long it takes!"

* * * * * * *

A week later Robert was still weak and helpless.

But he had discovered several important facts. First: the police had been called by June and had arrived in time to keep him from being killed. They had killed one of the three hoods and wounded another. The two surviving ones were in jail. Jake Turner had an iron-clad alibi and there wasn't any way of getting proof that he had been connected with the beating, except Robert's word—but he wasn't saying anything. The only conclusion that he could make was that there had been a pay-off.

Ruth Kirby had disappeared and there wasn't any trace of her to be found. June had done everything that she could to find the other woman, but it hadn't done her any good.

Robert Bradley had mixed emotions toward June.

She'd put her nose into his business and there wasn't any way of getting it out. She had saved his life; and that was one thing that he would never be able to pay her for. But, the main thing that he was concerned with was getting well and taking care of Jake Turner.

The police had questioned him and he'd given them just as much information as he had thought necessary.

"Yes, Jake Turner had done it."

"No, I don't know why."

"I'm sorry, but I don't know why!"

They hadn't believed him, naturally; it was a dumb story, but they couldn't make him talk, and that much he had on his side. Plus the fact that they didn't push too hard because of his condition.

There had been a police guard put on him, in fear that there might be another attempt on his life.

But that was as far as it went.

June was there every day to visit him and there was a slow sense of affection that built up between them. He needed a friend and she was openly offering herself.

Then the day came when he could leave the hospital if—and only if he kept in bed for a few more days. June Edmondson said that she'd take care of him, and nobody objected—least of all Robert—as long as he promised to take it easy for the next week.

He left the hospital a little over three weeks after he'd been put in.

CHAPTER SEVENTEEN

Robert Bradley didn't really know how to act with June. She had been with him every moment that she could. She had been there when he needed a friend; and what was more, she was responsible for saving his life. For that alone he owed her a lot.

As he lay in bed, half awake, thinking about the first three days out of the hospital, how she had been in the apartment every day and every night, jumping at his every call, he found it hard to organize his emotional response toward her. She had everything that a man might want in a woman. And the way she cared for him—he knew that she was falling in love with him. But, he didn't want things to develop in that direction.

Time moved slowly, yet he found his thoughts always returning to June—not Carol. And this sent stabs of guilt through him. June and her red hair and her beautiful, desirable body.

He didn't know how long he lay in bed before he heard the sound of movement in the other bedroom. The bedroom that Ruth Kirby had slept in for many nights before she had known June.

That was another thing he felt funny about. Living in the apartment where the brutal beating had taken place, but it was the only logical place to go.

The rent was paid for six months in advance. It had been the way Ruth Kirby had always arranged things. And, no doubt, the police were keeping a smart eye over him at this time. Plus, Jake Turner would be foolish to make any move so early on. The man would have been better off hiding away in a hole.

"Oh, hello, Bob!" June's voice interrupted his thoughts, as she walked across the room toward the side of his bed. She sat down next to him and gazed into his eyes. There was that longing in her expression that she did nothing to hide.

"Hi," was all he could say. It was the only thing that he felt like saying. Yet there was that pulsing desire in his guts that called for him to reach out and pull her to him. Angrily, he pushed away the thought and sat up.

June leaned close and kissed his cheek. "How are you feeling today?"

"Ready to jump out of bed and make a long dive into..." The words choked in his throat. His eyes had caught the opening at the top of June's bathrobe. There was the nice view of her round, full breasts. He could see the edge of their pink centers. For a moment he didn't move, not knowing what to do. He wanted to look away; but he couldn't. June had beautiful breasts. Circling, round, smooth-skinned, white, silky, and firm. The urge to reach out and place his fingers under that robe and feel the texture of her flesh was almost overwhelming.

June noticed the direction of his gaze and half smiled. "I see you are getting better!" she exclaimed, starting to stand.

"*No!* Wait!" he shouted. Then he wished he hadn't done it; he wished he had let her go.

For a long while they sat there, gazing at each other, not saying anything. He couldn't keep his eyes away from the opening at the top of her robe. It had parted more, and now he had a full view of her breasts. Desirable and alive. They were rising and falling with her breathing.

Suddenly he found his hand reaching involuntarily outwards, and then slowly his fingers slid under the robe, lightly touching the smooth surface of her skin. He wanted to pull his hand away, but he couldn't. He was overpowered by the nearness of this beautiful woman; a woman he knew he could have any time he asked; any time he made the effort to take her!

A tender, understanding expression moved across June's face as she looked at him. She didn't say anything, she didn't move closer or move away. She just sat there and let him touch her; let him caress her breasts.

Suddenly he didn't care any more. Carol was gone, and no matter how that hurt, there wasn't anything that he could do about it. Carol was dead, and June was alive and throbbing with passion and desire.

He reached for her, pulling her close and covering her lips with his.

A sigh broke from June, and her arms flung around his neck, crushing herself tightly against him, eagerly returning the kiss. Her lips, warm, trembling and parted, met his.

For a long time they clung to each other, breathing heavily. Then finally they relaxed and pressed their cheeks together. She sighed in his ear: "I thought you would never..."

That was the last thing they said to each other. She slid down alongside Robert and he slowly moved aside the robe, looking at the loveliness of her body. The naked wonder of it.

A pain caught in his throat; a pain of awe at the beauty of June. Her body was so perfect and so desirable and so sensual! He leaned down and kissed her throat and then her shoulder. A moment later he slid down further into the fullness of her breasts.

They made love wildly at first, anxiously, until exhaustion forced their muscles to relax. Then later they started again. This time tenderly, carefully, taking every sensation in, absorbing the very nearness and closeness of each other.

The next couple of days moved like a ribbon of red excitement across Robert's life. It was filled with kisses and caresses. Laughs and happiness. The only thing that kept it from being perfect was the inner knowledge of what he was doing and what a sin it was against Carol. But he kept that thought away from his consciousness, holding it down below the surface of awareness so that it couldn't bother him. He tried to forget for a while and live in the luxury of June's arms. He tried escaping in the sensual excitement of her and managed to find his momentary escape. But after escape comes reality. He couldn't run away from himself or his problems any more than he could run away from his body. He was attached to those problems, which were knotted around his life like a living web of evil, as strongly as his soul was attached to his body. There wasn't any escape from that, and even in June's arms he knew the truth, that soon he would have to face reality and either give up or fight again.

One month after the day of the beating, Robert woke in the morning with the sudden realization that the game was over and that now was the time to face up to the role that destiny had placed over his life. He had to stop the mental running and turn and take life in two strong hands and fight with it!

Slowly he sat up. He only gave a light, quick passing glance toward June, where she lay in the bed next to him, before standing and walking to the bathroom. In twenty minutes he was in the kitchen, sitting at the breakfast table and sipping black, strong coffee.

June stepped into the kitchen, a robe tied tightly around her.

"Hello, Bob," she said. But there was sadness in her voice, as if she sensed his mood. Slowly she poured herself a drink and then sat opposite him.

"What now?" she asked after a long silence.

"I guess you know?"

She nodded. "I've seen it for a day or two. Ever since you made love to me that first day...it was only a matter of time then. But you can't go out killing people."

"I've not decided that's what I'll do. There are a few things that I have to think out first."

"How are you going to get past the police guard?"

He shook his head, irritated. "That's no problem. They're only here to protect me from any other attempts. That's all."

"They think that you'll go after the man who did this."

149

"So, let them think!"

"Exactly what are...you going to do, Bob?"

"Play it by ear. First Turner. If I can get him alone, then.... Then we'll see."

Just then there was the ringing of the front door bell.

Robert looked questioningly at June and she returned the gaze, startled.

"Who's that?" he asked, stupidly.

June got up and walked into the living room to the front door. Opened it.

"Miss Edmondson, can I speak to Mr. Bradley? I'm from the D.A.'s office."

CHAPTER EIGHTEEN

The D.A. was a tall, thin man, with a small mustache that lined the top of his wide upper lip, bouncing with every word that he spoke. His first words of greetings were light and airy. "Well, Mr. Bradley, I've been wanting to meet you for some time, now. Please do sit down." He motioned with his hand first to the chair opposite on his desk.

Robert sat. There was a tightness in his guts ever since he'd been picked up by the D.A.'s men. Neither of the men who had brought him had said anything about what he was wanted for, and an inner terror had fluttered like a thousand winged insects in the pit of his stomach.

Now he looked at the man who was sitting opposite him, hands folded on the top of the desk. He saw a person who could be pleasant, and a man who could also be firm. It was a set face, lean and strong that stared back at him. The eyes were deep and gray.

"Well, I guess you wonder why you've been brought down here like this," the man finally said in his thin, high voice.

"You might put it that way," Robert countered tightly.

"Just a little questioning. We've been waiting

151

until you had a good chance to recover and think things over. From the answers you gave the police when you were in the hospital...well, they left something to be desired." The man smiled crookedly.

"I don't know what more I can tell you," Robert stated matter-of-factly.

"Oh, come on, Mr. Bradley, You can't really mean that!"

"I told the police everything I knew. I was invited up to Ruth Kirby's apartment and those men were there. They laid into me…. That's all I know."

The D.A.'s face hardened, becoming tight and drawn, serious and forceful. "Okay, if that's the way you feel about it, I guess I'll just have to be more direct!" He reached into the middle drawer of his desk and pulled out a folder. From it he took a paper. "Right here is a report on you, Mr. Bradley. It tells when you were born, everything you did until the time of your wife's death. It also says a few other things. I think that you should hear some of them." He paused, staring directly into Robert's eyes, a needle-sharp expression on his set face. Then he tapped the folder and said: "First: your wife was connected with a man called Dave Carlson. The Senate investigation decided to try using her as a witness, and Jake Turner was given orders to see to it that she was killed. She'd disappeared some months before—going back to her home town, Boise, married you. In some ways a very foolish move on her part. She should have realized that it was only a matter of time. But, then, people never want to believe they can be killed. They always believe there's a way out, a safe land, a fantasy place that never existed. She should have disappeared as a protected witness. Anything but just openly returning to her roots and getting married. Obviously she believed that these guys would think she really meant to remain silent. Simply by her being fairly open about her moves. But, well, they were afraid that she would talk and so they saw to it that she was put out of the picture. Then you disappeared and showed up here in Hollywood." He paused and looked up from the report. "Shall I continue?"

Robert had taken a deep breath of surprise at the information the D.A. had, and now he let it out in a sigh. "If you know that Jake Turner killed Carol...why haven't you arrested him?"

"For the same reason that we haven't arrested him for the little working over he gave you. We don't have any evidence!"

"How'd you find out about his connection with Carol's death?"

"We have our ways of getting information. But it is useless information without help from people like you. We can't *prove* that he did it. He had a good alibi—and the men he hired to do the job were out of town hoods with no other professional connection with Turner. Information isn't hard to get—it's proving it that is the difficulty. Because of people like you—and Miss Ruth Kirby. As you know she's disappeared, and we're afraid that she's been killed. We have no report from our informants on that. We know that orders have gone out for a hit on her—but no knowledge that it has been carried out. We can't find her, and I guess that the other side is having the same difficulty. She made a smart move and got lost."

"So what do you want me to do about it?"

Robert asked, a bitter edge on his voice. He knew what he had to do now. Stall. And then get at Turner and this man named Dave Carlson.

"Just tell us all that you know. Sign a complaint for the arrest of Jake Turner."

"I'm sorry, I can't do that!"

The D.A. dropped his eyes for a moment and then returned them to Robert's. "We know that you bribed a store keeper on Main Street to sell you a gun without a license. We could hold you on that..."

"I'm sorry, you'll have to hold me on that, then. I just don't have anything to add to my first report."

For a long time the D.A. didn't say anything, just sat there staring at Robert. Then finally he sighed and said: "Okay, play it your way. I'll give you twenty-four hours to make up your mind to change your attitude about this matter. Don't try to leave the town or you'll be slapped in jail." The man stood slowly. "Okay, get the hell out of here!" he snapped angrily.

The moment that Robert was outside he walked quickly to a taxi stand and jumped into the cab sitting there.

"Get moving," he said to the man, taking a twenty out of his pocket and handing it to the driver. "Get rid of my tail and there'll be another couple of twenties for you."

He knew that the D.A. had a plainclothesman following him, and that was the last thing he needed. First he had to be free to move without the police on his tail, and second he had to get to Turner, fast.

It took twenty minutes before the taxi-cab driver turned and said: "We've dropped the tail—now

154

where to, mister?"

Robert gave the man Turner's address and then settled back in his seat to think. He didn't really know what his plans were, exactly. All he planned, first, was to get hold of Turner and then let it all work out. He knew what he was bucking this time, and he wasn't going to take any chances. He had to get Turner alone—and when that happened he would know what to do next. How he planned on doing that, he wasn't sure. But he knew that one step at a time was all he could take; and that was what he was doing. Taking the first step.

* * * * * * *

The D.A. picked up the phone and said: "Yes?"

"*We* lost Bradley. He did everything in the book getting away from us."

"Okay, put out an all points net for him! In his condition he might do anything. All we need is another murder on our heads. He'll probably head for Turner or.... It shouldn't be hard to find him. But don't pick him up. Let him stir up a hornet's nest. He's in a position to explode the whole thing sky high—and that's what we've been needing!"

* * * * * * *

Turner looked at the man standing before him and frowned. "You mean to tell me that after four weeks you still haven't found any trace of Ruth Kirby?"

"Neither have the police!" the man reported.

"That doesn't matter. The thing is to get to her

before the police do."

"We traced her as far as Oakland, and then she just vanished." the man replied.

"Okay, then, just keep on it. And for god's sake get to her before the police. Carlson is on my back for this whole thing. He said I messed it up from beginning to end—and I'm afraid he's right. We have to clear it up. Things are getting tight in the Syndicate. The call-girl thing has already been pulled off the local boards as being too hot at this time. Later for that. Now the thing is to clamp down on the loose strings. Ruth Kirby is one big loose mouth. Bradley is to he left alone. Carlson doesn't want to be bothered with any more complications."

Just then the phone rang. Turner reached out and picked up the receiver. "Yes?"

"This is Carlson," the voice said in the receiver. "We've found the Kirby girl."

"What?" gasped Turner, feeling a sense of defeat.

"You've done the last bungling. There'll be repercussions. She's taken care of!" The phone clicked to silence.

Turner looked up at the other man, white-faced. His lips were tight and pale. "That was Carlson. They found Kirby..." He paused for a long while, not breathing. Then he stood, taking a deep breath.

"Now you get the hell out of here!" he snapped angrily.

He knew that he was washed up, and the only thing he could do now was pull out for good; leave the country. Disappear if possible. It might not do any good, but the least he could do was try. But one thought was strong in his mind as he left his office.

156

Before he left he was going to get the man who was responsible for the whole thing.

Kill Robert Bradley.

* * * * * * *

Robert had gone up to Turner's apartment, rang the bell, and waited for an answer. But there wasn't any answer. Only silence. Then he'd gone down to the cocktail lounge on the ground floor and ordered a scotch on the rocks.

He tried to think out what he was doing. He found himself thinking about what had happened in the few weeks he'd been in Hollywood. Everything that happened. And every time he thought back, the image of June kept coming before his mind's eye. And when he tried to replace that form with Carol's it became more and more difficult, as if his wife was slowly fading from his memory. Bitterly he finished the scotch and then ordered another. When it had been finished he paid the bill and then went to the lobby, where there was an office over the door that said: *Manager.* He rang the bell and then waited. A man answered it after a moment. "Yes?"

"I was wondering if you knew how to get hold of Mr. Turner."

The man looked strangely at him for a moment and then said, "Why, Mr. Turner just checked out about two hours ago. Gave me a month's rent in advance and then left."

Robert didn't wait to hear the rest. The only thing that was left was to look up the name *Dave Carlson* in the phone book.

Five minutes later he was in a phone booth, a

sense of utter defeat moving through him. There wasn't any Dave Carlson. Tired, he moved from the booth and stepped across the large lobby and out onto the street. There was nothing that he could do now but go back to the apartment and think things out. What good that would do, he didn't have the least idea. But he would worry about that later. He was at a dead-end, and strangely there was a feeling of inner relief. He'd done everything that he could...and that hadn't been enough.

Twenty minutes later he parked his car in the garage under the apartment house. Killed the engine and then walked into the building, into the elevator and a few minutes later down the hall toward the rooms where June and he had spent the last days together.

As he opened the door he heard a woman's voice call out desperately.

"Run! Get away!" It was June.

Then another voice that he quickly recognized: "Don't make that mistake, Bradley! I'll kill her!"

It was Turner.

158

CHAPTER NINETEEN

Robert stepped slowly into the apartment, closing the door behind him. Suddenly every ounce of resistance and fight had left him. He felt sick inside; sweat started ebbing from every pore in him. He just looked across the room, stony-faced.

Jake Turner was sitting on the modern, low Chinese sofa, a cold ugly stub-nosed .38 in his hands. He had a twisted grin on his features. "Well, I've been waiting for you, sucker. But really not too long."

June rushed to Robert's side. "Oh, God, Bob, why didn't you run?"

"I couldn't leave you here."

"Your long trail ended—hasn't it, Mr. Bradley?" Turner sighed, slowly standing, keeping the gun pointed in Robert's direction.

"I guess so. We meet again under the same conditions."

"Not quite. This time I'm going to finish the job that my men seemed to have muffed." His face became serious; a deadly hardness coming across his features.

"What do you want to kill me for?" Robert asked, trying to stall for time. He didn't really care so much about his own life—he just wanted to take

Jake Turner with him; and save June.

"Well, now. Aren't you the bright boy? You want to know why I want to kill you? Well that's not so hard to figure," Turner snarled, slowly stepping forward. "If it hadn't been for you snooping around, everything would have gone along very nicely. But you seem to have put a real big stumbling block in our way. Because of your large over-sized nose, the Syndicate has put a stopper to a very, very large deal, and because of you getting in my way, you might say that I've been put in a very bad position." Anger choked Turner. "You're goddam nose has smelled up the whole deal. Now the big boys are out to pull the rug out from under *me*—but I'm going to see that you go down with me!"

"Oh, come on, I couldn't have caused all that trouble," Robert said, trying to make his voice sound casual; trying at all costs to delay the end to the last moment; to give himself a chance, any chance at all, to save June.

"Don't fool yourself, Bradley," Turner snapped, coming to a stop a few yards from him and June. "It's not you. *Ruth Kirby*. She's the one that really got me into trouble, I set her up for a good share of the new deal and because of you—and her damn attempts to save you from this very end—she made a very bad mistake, and because of it *I looked bad!* The Syndicate doesn't like mistakes—and mine was in backing her. Carlson didn't like it. Oh, they probably won't try to kill me—they'll just let me escape from the country. That's the way they work. They just don't want me in on any more deals here. I'm black-balled from here on. But Ruth got hers!" His mood changed, and he motioned with the gun.

160

"Okay, let's get out of here. I'm taking you two for a long, one way ride!"

"Let June go!" Robert demanded, desperately.

Turner laughed. "You kidding? This time I won't be leaving *anybody* behind to mess things up. When I leave, I want to be clear! And you two are in my way now."

Robert sighed and turned, moving toward the door. He opened it and started through as Turner put the gun in his pocket, keeping his hand on it. "Don't make the mistake of thinking that I won't use this if it is necessary! Even in broad daylight!"

The three of them moved down the hall to the elevator. A little later they were gliding down to the ground floor. All the time Robert was trying to think of some way to jump Turner; some way to change the situation so that he could blow that dirty bastard's brains out!

They walked out of the elevator, across the lobby, and out onto the street.

"This way," Turner indicated, moving toward the end of the block. "That car—the blue one at the end. Get in it—you behind the driver's seat, Bradley. I'll sit in the back seat with your little girl friend here."

A few minutes later they were driving along the street toward the freeway.

"Where are we going?" Robert asked, tensely.

"Oh, don't you worry about that. Just north on the freeway. That's all you have to worry about. But remember, one mistaken move behind the wheel and *she* gets it first!"

A cold icy chill ran down Robert's spine. He felt a shiver move through his body. He *had* to get June out of the situation. If it weren't for her he would run the car into a wall, killing both Turner and himself. He found himself very concerned about June Edmondson. A month before it wouldn't have mattered to him; but now it did. And that fact startled him. He didn't want anything to happen to June. And it wasn't just because he owed her so much. It went deeper than that. Not love, he was sure of that; but it was an emotion very close to love. Affection at least, coupled with...with something that he didn't quite understand.

They drove for about twenty or thirty minutes, then Turner told him to turn off the freeway, onto Van Nuys Boulevard. Then they drove for about fifteen minutes longer before Turner told him to turn left. They had gone through the town of Van Nuys. They drove for more than two hours, leaving the San Fernando Valley and beyond Chatsworth and out into Simi Valley. Then he was directed along a lonely country road, rutted and unpaved. Finally they came to another turn-off and he was told to make a left. After five minutes they came to a small farm house that was quietly waiting for them.

"That will do!" Turner demanded, opening the back door and getting out. Then he motioned the other two out. "Into the house—and fast!"

"What makes you think you'll get away with this?" Robert demanded, as they stepped into the old house and Turner closed the door behind them.

"Nobody around here to find you. You won't be found for months—if ever! And nobody will hear the gunshots. We're far away from everything and everybody. There isn't a soul within a couple of miles in any direction of here."

Just then there was the sound of footsteps in another room in the house and then two men stepped into the front room, one of them carrying a submachine gun pointed at the three of them.

"What the hell!" Turner gasped.

The man standing weaponless grinned: "Carlson thought you might run out here. You know that the boss don't like people running out on him. So he just put a few stakeouts at key points."

"You're kidding?" Turner choked in terror.

"We're deadly serious. You made a very big mistake, and it's caused the Syndicate a setback in its plans. The boys don't like that. They don't like it at all!"

While the three hoods were talking, Robert had slid slightly to one side, waiting to take advantage of this setback in Turner's plans.

Suddenly all hell broke loose!

Turner pointed his gun and fired, before anybody could move. The bullet whipped the man carrying the Tommy-gun completely around, smashing him into the far wall.

Robert leaped forward, half diving through the air toward the Tommy-gun and hoping that the two other men were too busy with each other to react to his action.

There was the sound of a second shot as Robert's hand grasped the gun and pulled it to him, at the same time twisting around toward the other two men.

Turner was standing, smoke drifting up from the barrel of the small .38, a tense expression on his face. The gun was pointed at Robert. But the submachine gun was already centered on the man's

163

stomach.

For a long while the two of them stared at each other, Turner's face growing whiter and whiter. Finally his lips parted as if to say something and then hung open, unmoving.

"Looks like a deadlock, Turner," Robert stated in a tight voice. "But the only thing is that I have the advantage in two ways. I'm sure to get you. And even if you do hit me, I might survive—*but you won't!*"

"So...let's call...call it off!" Turner cried in a shaking voice, his eyes wide with terror.

"Oh, no, now I wouldn't do that!" Robert said grimly, slowly starting to rise to his feet.

"What's the point? I'm a good shot," Turner retorted, gaining some self-control, finally. "I'll just kill you.

"That's the point, Turner. *I don't care.* I'm not afraid to die! But you are!"

For a long time Turner stared at Robert, not saying anything. He was waiting out the game; a game of bluff from his point of view.

Finally Robert said lightly, "Either fire or drop the gun, Turner. Drop it—or fire. I'll give you to the count of three, then I'm going to blow the holy crap out of you, if you haven't dropped it."

Turner's eyes widened, becoming bright. Sweat formed on his forehead. "You don't bluff me!"

"One!"

"What about this girl friend of yours?" Turner asked, suddenly, jerking the barrel in her direction.

"You want her to go with me?"

Only for a moment did Robert hesitate. *"Two!"*

Robert's finger tightened on the trigger and his

jaw set.

"How do I know you would let me live?" Turner said evenly. "I don't have any course but to take her with me!"

"That's the chance you'll have to take!"

"You don't want *her* to die, do you?" Turner grinned. But the grin froze as Robert started to say—*"Three!"*

Turner's gun clattered to the floor before the word had been finished.

Robert relaxed, relieved. At that last moment he had had that sickening feeling that he might not be able to pull the trigger. But he never would know for sure now. The test was over and he'd won the game. But there was something else that had to be done, first.

"Don't kill me!" Turner pleaded frantically, almost screaming out the words. "Please, *don't kill me!*"

June rushed up to him: "It's not worth it!" she told him. "It's not worth it!"

"Okay, Turner, it's up to you. I want a confession. The complete details of my wife's death. Everything!"

"You can't make me do that!" Turner cried in terror. Sweat was making his face shiny.

"Write it or I'll kill you."

"But that will kill me, too! I wouldn't have a chance!" the man pleaded.

"You'll have a better chance than Carol had. A hell of a lot better one. With a smart lawyer—who knows, you might get off easy...with a life sentence."

"Write it or I'll pull this trigger!" Robert's fin-

ger tightened, lowering the barrel of the Tommy-
gun at the pit of Turners stomach. "And I'll see to it
that you die slow!"

Turner gasped.

"Make up your mind, Mister Big Shot! I'll give
you the count to three to make up your mind!"

"No!" Turner cried. "Okay. I'll do what you
say.... Anyway, if I go, I might as well pull Carlson
with me!"

* * * * * * *

It was twelve long, tiring hours later that Robert
and June pulled up in a taxi to the front of the
apartment where they had been staying.

Robert looked at June for a moment and smiled,
then the two of them stepped from the cab. He paid
the bill and they walked up to the apartment building.

A lot had happened in the few hours since they
had been there before. Turner's confession had tied
up everything into a nice neat package. There was a
warrant for the arrest of Carlson, and the D.A. had
the complete cooperation of Jake Turner in ex-
change for a promise to get him off with a life sentence. That meant the Syndicate boys were in trouble!

But, except for the coming trials, that was part
of the future. An uncertain future, and yet one that
Robert felt would take care of itself. A lot had happened, much too fast for him to take it all in and see
where it left him.

But one thing he knew: what he had come to Hollywood for had been finished and successful. He'd gotten Carol's killers.

And something else had happened. *June Edmondson.*

As they closed the apartment door behind them, June moved into his arms.

"What a day," she sighed, brushing her lips along his neck and pressing herself closer to him. Then suddenly they were tenderly kissing.

The feel of her body; the supple give and sensual excitement of it faded out all thoughts for a few moments. Then they pulled away and looked at each other.

"What now, Bob?" June asked.

"A shower and then a little sleep!"

She laughed. She knew he realized that wasn't what she meant. She wanted to know where June Edmondson stood in his future.

He already knew the answer to that question: she stood strong and tall. If nothing else, Robert had learned one thing about life: let the dead remain dead.

Carol's life had been filled with nightmare years and a short few happy days as his wife. But all of that was past. She had live in hell in Hollywood.

June had managed to escape that kind of existence.

June turned half sadly, starting to move away.

"Wait a minute!" he told her, reaching out and pulling her closer.

"I think I want to continue that!" he said, kissing her lips.

A moment later he lifted her in his arms and started for the bedroom.

"You know," he told her, as they lay down, locked in each other's arms, "I'm going to want to continue this for a very long, long time."

She smiled up at him, contentedly.

"I hope that's a very long time, my love," she murmured softly in his ear.

"I believe that depends on you," he promised.

"Then it will be very long."

Suddenly neither of them was saying anything anymore. Not for a very long, long time!

ABOUT THE AUTHOR

Charles Nuetzel was born in San Francisco in 1934, and writes:

"As long as I can remember I wanted to be a writer. It was a dream I never thought would materialize. But with the help of Forrest J Ackerman, who became my agent, I managed to finally make it into print.

"I was lucky enough not only in selling my work to publishers but also ending up packaging books for some of them, and finally becoming a 'publisher' much like those who had bought my first novels. From there it as a simple leap to editing not only a science-fiction anthology, but also a line of SF books for Powell Sci-Fi back in the 1960s. Throughout these active professional years I had the chance to design some covers and do graphic cover layouts for pocket books & magazines."

Much of his work in covers and graphics are a result of having had a father who was a professional commercial artist, and who did a number of covers for sci-fi magazines in the 1950s and later for pocket books—even for some of Mr. Nuetzel's books.

In retirement he has become involved in swing dancing, a long time lover of Big Band jazz. But more interestingly world travels have taken him (and his wife Brigitte) across the world, to Hawaii, Caribbean, Mexico, Kenya, Egypt, Peru, having a lifelong interest in ancient civilizations. His website is full of thousands of pictures taken during these trips.